MORAY D

THE ART SCHO

KATHERINE DALTON RENOIR ('Moray Dalton') was born in Hammersmith, London in 1881, the only child of a Canadian father and English mother.

The author wrote two well-received early novels, *Olive in Italy* (1909), and *The Sword of Love* (1920). However, her career in crime fiction did not begin until 1924, after which Moray Dalton published twenty-nine mysteries, the last in 1951. The majority of these feature her recurring sleuths, Scotland Yard inspector Hugh Collier and private inquiry agent Hermann Glide.

Moray Dalton married Louis Jean Renoir in 1921, and the couple had a son a year later. The author lived on the south coast of England for the majority of her life following the marriage. She died in Worthing, West Sussex, in 1963.

Moray Dalton Mysteries
Available from Dean Street Press

MORAY DALTON

THE ART SCHOOL MURDERS

With an introduction by Curtis Evans

DEAN STREET PRESS

LOST GOLD FROM A GOLDEN AGE

The Detective Fiction of Moray Dalton
(Katherine Mary Deville Dalton Renoir, 1881-1963)

"GOLD" COMES in many forms. For literal-minded people gold may be merely a precious metal, physically stripped from the earth. For fans of Golden Age detective fiction, however, gold can be artfully spun out of the human brain, in the form not of bricks but books. While the father of Katherine Mary Deville Dalton Renoir may have derived the Dalton family fortune from nuggets of metallic ore, the riches which she herself produced were made from far humbler, though arguably ultimately mightier, materials: paper and ink. As the mystery writer Moray Dalton, Katherine Dalton Renoir published twenty-nine crime novels between 1924 and 1951, the majority of which feature her recurring sleuths, Scotland Yard inspector Hugh Collier and private inquiry agent Hermann Glide. Although the Moray Dalton mysteries are finely polished examples of criminally scintillating Golden Age art, the books unjustifiably fell into neglect for decades. For most fans of vintage mystery they long remained, like the fabled Lost Dutchman's mine, tantalizingly elusive treasure. Happily the crime fiction of Moray Dalton has been unearthed for modern readers by those industrious miners of vintage mystery at Dean Street Press.

Born in Hammersmith, London on May 6, 1881, Katherine was the only child of Joseph Dixon Dalton and Laura Back Dalton. Like the parents of that admittedly more famous mistress of mystery, Agatha Christie, Katherine's parents hailed from different nations, separated by the Atlantic Ocean. While both authors had British mothers, Christie's father was American and Dalton's father Canadian.

Laura Back Dalton, who at the time of her marriage in 1879 was twenty-six years old, about fifteen years younger than her husband, was the daughter of Alfred and Catherine Mary Back. In her early childhood years Laura Back resided at Valley House, a lovely regency villa built around 1825 in Stratford St. Mary, Suffolk, in the heart of so-called "Constable Country" (so named for the fact that the great Suffolk landscape artist John Constable painted many of his works in and around Stratford). Alfred Back was a wealthy miller who with his brother Octavius, a corn merchant, owned and operated a steam-powered six-story mill right across the River Stour from Valley House. In 1820 John Constable, himself the son of a miller, executed a painting of fishers on the River Stour which partly included the earlier, more modest incarnation (complete with water wheel) of the Back family's mill. (This piece Constable later repainted under the title *The Young Waltonians*, one of his best known works.) After Alfred Back's death in 1860, his widow moved with her daughters to Brondesbury Villas in Maida Vale, London, where Laura in the 1870s met Joseph Dixon Dalton, an eligible Canadian-born bachelor and retired gold miner of about forty years of age who lived in nearby Kew.

Joseph Dixon Dalton was born around 1838 in London, Ontario, Canada, to Henry and Mary (Dixon) Dalton, Wesleyan Methodists from northern England who had migrated to Canada a few years previously. In 1834, not long before Joseph's birth, Henry Dalton started a soap and candle factory in London, Ontario, which after his death two decades later was continued, under the appellation Dalton Brothers, by Joseph and his siblings Joshua and Thomas. (No relation to the notorious "Dalton Gang" of American outlaws is presumed.) Joseph's sister Hannah wed John Carling, a politician who came from a prominent family of Canadian brewers and was later knighted for his varied public services, making him Sir John and his wife Lady Hannah. Just how Joseph left the family soap and candle business to prospect for gold is currently unclear, but sometime in the 1870s, after fabulous gold rushes at Cariboo and Cassiar, British Columbia and the Black Hills of South Dakota, among other locales, Joseph left Canada and carried his riches with him to London, England, where for a time he enjoyed life as a gentleman of leisure in one of the great metropolises of the world.

Although Joshua and Laura Dalton's first married years were spent with their daughter Katherine in Hammersmith at a villa named Kenmore Lodge, by 1891 the family had moved to 9 Orchard Place in Southampton, where young Katherine received a private education from Jeanne Delport, a governess from Paris. Two decades later, Katherine, now 30 years old, resided with her parents at Perth Villa in the village of Merriott, Somerset, today about an eighty miles' drive west of Southampton. By this time Katherine had published, under the masculine-sounding pseudonym of Moray Dalton (probably a gender-bending play on "Mary Dalton") a well-received first novel, *Olive in Italy* (1909), a study of a winsome orphaned Englishwoman attempting to make her own living as an artist's model in Italy that possibly had been influenced by E.M. Forster's novels *Where Angels Fear to Tread* (1905) and *A Room with a View* (1908), both of which are partly set in an idealized Italy of pure gold sunlight and passionate love. Yet despite her accomplishment, Katherine's name had no occupation listed next it in the census two years later.

During the Great War the Daltons, parents and child, resided at 14 East Ham Road in Littlehampton, a seaside resort town located 19 miles west of Brighton. Like many other bookish and patriotic British women of her day, Katherine produced an effusion of memorial war poetry, including "To Some Who Have Fallen," "Edith Cavell," "Rupert Brooke," "To Italy" and "Mort Homme." These short works appeared in the *Spectator* and were reprinted during and after the war in George Herbert Clarke's *Treasury of War Poetry* anthologies. "To Italy," which Katherine had composed as a tribute to the beleaguered British ally after its calamitous defeat, at the hands of the forces of Germany and Austria-Hungary, at the Battle of Caporetto in 1917, even popped up in the United States in the "poet's corner" of the *United Mine Workers Journal*, perhaps on account of the poem's pro-Italy sentiment, doubtlessly agreeable to Italian miner immigrants in America.

Katherine also published short stories in various periodicals, including *The Cornhill Magazine*, which was then edited by Leonard Huxley, son of the eminent zoologist Thomas Henry Huxley and father of famed writer Aldous Huxley. Leonard Huxley obligingly read over--and in his words "plied my scalpel upon"--Katherine's second novel, *The Sword of Love*, a romantic adventure saga set in the Florentine Republic at the time of Lorenzo the Magnificent and the infamous Pazzi Conspiracy, which was published in 1920. Katherine writes with obvious affection for *il bel paese* in her first two novels and her poem "To Italy," which concludes with the ringing lines

> Greece was enslaved, and Carthage is but dust,
> But thou art living, maugre [i.e., in spite of] all thy
>   scars,
> To bear fresh wounds of rapine and of lust,
> Immortal victim of unnumbered wars.
> Nor shalt thou cease until we cease to be
> Whose hearts are thine, beloved Italy.

The author maintained her affection for "beloved Italy" in her later Moray Dalton mysteries, which include sympathetically-rendered Italian settings and characters.

Around this time Katherine in her own life evidently discovered romance, however short-lived. At Brighton in the spring of 1921, the author, now nearly 40 years old, wed a presumed Frenchman, Louis Jean Renoir, by whom the next year she bore her only child, a son, Louis Anthony Laurence Dalton Renoir. (Katherine's father seems to have missed these important developments in his daughter's life, apparently having died in 1918, possibly in the flu pandemic.) Sparse evidence as to the actual existence of this man, Louis Jean Renoir, in Katherine's life suggests that the marriage may not have been a successful one. In the 1939 census Katherine was listed as living with her mother Laura at 71 Wallace Avenue in Worthing, Sussex, another coastal town not far from Brighton, where she had married Louis Jean eighteen years earlier; yet he is not in evidence, even though he is stated to be Katherine's husband in her mother's will, which was probated in Worthing in 1945. Perhaps not unrelatedly, empathy with what people in her day considered unorthodox sexual unions characterizes the crime fiction which Katherine would write.

Whatever happened to Louis Jean Renoir, marriage and motherhood did not slow down "Moray Dalton." Indeed, much to the contrary, in 1924, only a couple of years after the birth of her son, Katherine published, at the age of 42 (the same age at which P.D. James published her debut mystery novel, *Cover Her Face*), *The Kingsclere Mystery*, the first of her 29 crime novels. (Possibly the title was derived from the village of Kingsclere, located some 30 miles north of Southampton.) The heady scent of Renaissance romance which perfumes *The Sword of Love* is found as well in the first four Moray Dalton mysteries (aside from *The Kingsclere Mystery*, these are *The Shadow on the Wall, The Black Wings* and *The Stretton Darknesse Mystery*), which although set in the present-day world have, like much of the mystery fiction of John Dickson Carr, the elevated emotional temperature of the highly-colored age of the cavaliers. However in 1929 and 1930, with the publication of, respectively, *One by One They Disappeared*, the first of the Inspector Hugh Collier mysteries and *The Body in the Road*, the debut Hermann Glide tale, the Moray Dalton novels begin to become more typical of British crime fiction at that time, ultimately bearing considerable similarity to the work of Agatha Christie and Dorothy L. Sayers, as well as other prolific women mystery authors who would achieve popularity in the 1930s, such as Margery Allingham, Lucy Beatrice Malleson (best known as "Anthony Gilbert") and Edith Caroline Rivett, who wrote under the pen names E.C.R. Lorac and Carol Carnac.

For much of the decade of the 1930s Katherine shared the same publisher, Sampson Low, with Edith Rivett, who published her first detective novel in 1931, although Rivett moved on, with both of her pseudonyms, to that rather more prominent purveyor of mysteries, the Collins Crime Club. Consequently the Lorac and Carnac novels are better known today than those of Moray Dalton. Additionally, only three early Moray Dalton titles (*One by One They Disappeared, The Body in the Road* and *The Night of Fear*) were picked up in the United States, another factor which mitigated against the Dalton mysteries achieving long-term renown. It is also possible that the independently wealthy author, who left an estate valued, in modern estimation, at nearly a million American dollars at her death at the age of 81 in 1963, felt less of an imperative to "push" her writing than the typical "starving author."

Whatever forces compelled Katherine Dalton Renoir to write fiction, between 1929 and 1951 the author as Moray Dalton published fifteen Inspector Hugh Collier mysteries and ten other crime novels (several of these with Hermann Glide). Some of the non-series novels daringly straddle genres. *The Black Death*, for example, somewhat bizarrely yet altogether compellingly merges the murder mystery with post-apocalyptic science fiction, whereas *Death at the Villa*, set in Italy during the Second World War, is a gripping wartime adventure thriller with crime and death. Taken together, the imaginative and ingenious Moray Dalton crime fiction, wherein death is not so much a game as a dark and compelling human drama, is one of the more significant bodies of work by a Golden Age mystery writer—though the author has, until now, been most regrettably overlooked by publishers, for decades remaining accessible almost solely to connoisseurs with deep pockets.

Even noted mystery genre authorities Jacques Barzun and Wendell Hertig Taylor managed to read only five books by Moray Dalton, all of which the pair thereupon listed in their massive critical compendium, *A Catalogue of Crime* (1972; revised and expanded 1989). Yet Barzun and Taylor were warm admirers of the author's writing, avowing for example, of the twelfth Hugh Collier mystery, *The Condamine Case* (under the impression that the author was a man): "[T]his is the author's 17th book, and [it is] remarkably fresh and unstereotyped [actually it was Dalton's 25th book, making it even more remarkable—C.E.]. . . . [H]ere is a neglected man, for his earlier work shows him to be a conscientious workman, with a flair for the unusual, and capable of clever touches."

Today in 2019, nine decades since the debut of the conscientious and clever Moray Dalton's Inspector Hugh Collier detective series, it is a great personal pleasure to announce that this criminally neglected woman is neglected no longer and to welcome her books back into light. Vintage crime fiction fans have a golden treat in store with the classic mysteries of Moray Dalton.

The Art School Murders

A blackout during war, or in preparation for an expected war, is the practice of collectively mini-mizing outdoor light. . . . to prevent crews of enemy aircraft from being able to identify their targets by sight. . . .

"Blackout," *Wikipedia*

"I'm worried. . . . This damned blackout. I'm afraid of what may happen in the dark."

Inspector Hugh Collier in *The Art School Murders* (1943), by Moray Dalton

IF THE malevolent unknown who savagely slew five women in London in 1888--forever known to his "public," if you will, as "Jack the Ripper"--has ever conversed in Hell with Gordon Frederick Cummins, executed for the monstrous murders of four women which took place in wartime London in February 1942, perhaps they have discussed the capriciousness of fame (or more accurately notoriety), which made the one depraved maniac eternally famous while allowing the other quickly to become largely forgotten.

Part of the reason for this disparity in renown is the fact that the Ripper was never caught. Indeed his (?) identity remains unknown, fueling endless speculation and theories in books, articles and internet postings. Conversely, Gordon Cummins was quickly apprehended by police and executed for his terrible killings. The jury deliberated for only thirty-five minutes before finding him guilty as charged, and he was hanged on June 25, only two months after his trial.

Of course the fact that Britain was fighting a war for survival around the world that deadly week when Gordon Cummins violently prowled in London had something to do with it too. What were the deaths of four obscure London women--horrific as those deaths had been--compared to the manifold calamities--the mayhem and mass slaughter--going on around the world?

Nevertheless, the killings made quite a stir. There was much talk about how the blackout had made Londoners, particularly women, less safe by making it easier for villains to commit heinous crimes under cover of the night. Ill deeds done in darkness, don't you know. Gordon Cummins was only caught because he left his registered gas mask behind after fleeing from the scene of an interrupted attack he had made on a woman. As a newspaper put it, Cummins' target "might have been killed but for the sudden appearance of a small boy with a flashlight."

Whatever its deleterious impact on society, the blackout certainly proved a boon to mystery writers. In 1940 there came *The Black-Out Murders*, a novel by the ever-opportunistic crime writer Leonard Gribble, who after the war would blast his readers with *Atomic Murder* (1947). Then there was J. Russell Warren's *Gas-Mask Murder* from 1939, which, when it was published in the United States the next year was re-titled, yes, *Murder in the Blackout*. The blackout also appeared in Gladys Mitchell's *Brazen Tongue*, likewise published in 1940.

Classic genteel detection, either in print or on film, could never encompass the bloody horror of the "Blackout Ripper," who it was reported, had sexually mutilated some of his victims with a can opener, but in 1943, there appeared a disappointingly dull "Poverty Row" (i.e., cheapie) American mystery film, scripted by Curt Siodmak, called *London Blackout Murders*, which specifically references Jack the Ripper, as well as a fine mystery novel by Moray Dalton, the title of which--*The Art School Murders*--gave no hint of its wartime setting, though it was, I believe, the author's only mystery actually published during the war.

Although sometimes erroneously listed as a non-series mystery, *The Art School Murders* is in fact an Inspector Hugh Collier story—by my reckoning the tenth of fifteen Collier tales. It is an excellent detective novel, representative of the author's more stripped-down post-war, proto police procedural style. Certainly it is reminiscent of works by the four major Crime Queens (Christie, Sayers, Marsh and Allingham), with its overall genteel setting and its keen-eyed social observation; yet it has a bit of a sharper edge, I think, than much of the Crime Queens' work, lacking in the little snobberies and petty condescensions often associated with their fiction.

Yet Dalton's Hugh Collier, while a more believable cop than Ngaio Marsh's oh-so-impossibly-exquisite Roderick Alleyn, is cut as well from genteel (though not aristocratic) cloth, being one of those attractive, kindly, charming and gentlemanly police detectives whom we associate with the major and minor British Crime Queens. (He especially reminds me of E.C.R. Lorac's Inspector Macdonald.) One of the lines in the book says of Collier that "Crude manners always put him on his mettle." This is typical of a Golden Age fictional sleuth, as imagined by the Crime Queens. Not to mention vastly different from today's depressing viral American cop videos, where every other word that seemingly gets uttered by one of Our Men in Blue begins with an "F" and ends with a "K" or "G."

It is a pleasure to accompany Hugh Collier as he politely but persistently pursues and finally brings to justice a particularly nasty killer, one who over the course of the story murders three women in the London suburbs, two of them for an exceedingly callous reason. Dalton gets right down to business, producing her first dead body on page four. Scotland Yard, as embodied by Hugh Collier, enters ten pages later. The main setting of the novel is an art school founded by a highly regarded though hugely egocentric native Italian portrait painter, Aldo Morosini. The initial murder victim is Althea Greville, a luscious though somewhat long in the tooth blonde (she is over forty), who until her stabbing death served as a life model at the school. Two more murder victims follow (one of them a female student at the school, who is stabbed to death at a cinema). Finally, however, Collier selects the right piece in the puzzle and identifies the culprit.

I use the term puzzle piece advisedly because four-fifths of the way through the novel the author herself writes this of Collier's thought process:

> As he pondered his notes on the case he had a worrying feeling that he had missed something, that he had picked up the false clues and left the one that really mattered trailing. Was there anything to be gained by turning back? In all these statements taken from the students at the school, the staff of the cinema, was there one revealing sentence, one operative word that had been passed over, unnoticed at the time?

Yes, dear reader, there was! Can you find it before Collier?

Collier pursues a fairly limited number of suspects, in contrast with those Golden Age country house mysteries where absurdly there are about a dozen guests (or more) staying for the weekend (though there is only one bathroom—see the detective's "rough sketch"), all of whom had some motivation to have bludgeoned the baronet at midnight in his study. Despite her circumscribed field, however, Dalton still manages to put quite a bit of suspense into the telling.

Dalton also presents her lower, middle and upper class characters alike as real human beings, something which did not always happen in vintage British mystery, which often portrayed lower class people in comically demeaning fashion. In *The Art School Murders*, however, it is the frostily conventional genteel aunt who hardly misses her murdered niece, in contrast with the old family servant, Emma, who feels the young woman's absence keenly. We, the readers, are invited by the author to empathize as well.

Aside from the blackout bits in Dalton's novel, there are some other nice details for readers of vintage mystery who enjoy social history as well as murder puzzles, primarily concerning the influence of American culture on wartime Britain, a subject which drew the dismayed interest of George Orwell, among other prominent English commentators of the day. The murdered art student is a great fan of American films, particularly comparative "oldies" starring Fred Astaire and Ginger Rogers. "She's got what they call a pash on that Fred Astaire," explains the maid Emma. "I heard her humming one of the tunes. She's got a record of it. 'The Way You Look Tonight.'" The young woman's murder discordantly occurs at a showing of the classic 1936 Fred and Ginger film *Swing Time*. Meanwhile Collier's assistant, burly Sergeant Duffield, "goes regularly to the pictures with his wife on his evenings off duty" and is "gradually acquiring a transatlantic vocabulary." Collier, we learn to our amusement, looks "forward hopefully to the time when his sergeant would refer to his colleagues as bulls."

In 1930 and 1931 three of Moray Dalton's crime novels had been published in the United States, yet over the next two decades, the remainder of her writing career, none were. Dalton stopped writing, as far as we know, in 1951, and she was soon forgotten, though the discerning Jacques Barzun and Wendell Hertig Taylor praised her highly in their *Catalogue of Crime*. Was Dalton disappointed with the relative lack of success of her books? I do not know, but she certainly had every right to be, for in my estimation she produced (I will say it again) some of the finest British crime fiction of mid-century. Sometimes writers, often women, never receive their dues in their lifetimes (just think of the fantastically egregious cases of Jane Austen and Emily Dickinson), but occasionally time redresses the balance. I hope that such happens in the strange case of the proverbially "unjustly neglected" Moray Dalton.

Curtis Evans

CHAPTER I
RED PAINT

AT TWENTY minutes past eight, Mrs. Pearce came out of the cottage at the entrance to the school grounds and trudged up the cinder path to the main door. It was the caretaker's job to open up and air the classrooms before the students arrived, and to clean out and refuel the stove in the life classroom, where the temperature was supposed to be maintained at about seventy degrees for the benefit of the model, but he was an ex-soldier who had been badly gassed in 1917, and during the winter months his patient and much enduring little wife did most of his work.

It was a cold, sunless November morning, with a ground mist lying like a grey blanket over the rain-sodden fields, and Mrs. Pearce's numbed fingers were slow in turning the key in the lock. There were three letters on the mat. She picked them up and put them on the desk in the secretary's office on the right of the door as she went in.

"Hallo Mrs. Pearce!"

"Oh sir! Oh Mr. Kent! You did give me a start—"

"Sorry," said Kent. He looked at her rather curiously, noticing that she had gone rather white about the lips. "You shouldn't be carrying that heavy scuttle. Where's Pearce?"

"He's got one of his bad turns, sir. His chest—"

Kent grunted. He had not a very big opinion of the caretaker, but it was not his business. "When does Miss Roland turn up usually?"

It was Mrs. Pearce's turn to register contempt. "Her? Not a minute before she has to."

"I see. Well, I think one of those letters may be for me. Yes, it is. All right, Mrs. Pearce, carry on."

Mrs. Pearce shuffled away down the passage, a small subfusc figure swathed in her hessian apron, leaving Kent leaning against the pitch pine partition that shut off the cubby hole called the staff room from the secretary's office while he read his letter.

"Queer," she thought. "Why should he be having letters sent here? A bit of fluff? I wouldn't have said Mr. Kent was that sort, but you can't never tell. Something he don't want that Nosy Parker of a sister of his to know about. Trying to find another job maybe. I wouldn't blame him. This place is a dead end and no blooming error."

Only two new students last term, and seven had left without waiting to be passed out of the preliminary class into the life. That showed. The fact was that Mr. Morosini had lost interest. He left the teaching to Mr. Kent and Mr. Hollis and hardly ever came near the place himself. "I give it another year," Mrs. Pearce told herself pessimistically, "and then Tom and me'll be out. What hopes. I'll live to be glad little Ellie died of them measles."

John Kent slipped his letter into the side pocket of his shabby tweed sports coat and took a cigarette from his case. He knew even better than Mrs. Pearce that the Morosini school, never indigenous in that soil, was a dying plant. Plant, he thought cynically, was the right word, for the fees were absurdly high, and what could he and Hollis give the students that they couldn't get at a municipal art school? Models every day admittedly, instead of only two or three times a week, and a greater choice of models; and of course, the kudos that still attached to the name of Morosini. And there was the fact that two of his favourite pupils in the early days, when the school was a new toy, had achieved a resounding success. Joyce Bailey had arrived with 'The Dancer in Yellow', and Heronshaw with his 'Whelkstall'. Morosini had seen to it that their pictures were hung on the line. In those days he had talked of building a school that would be worthy of his ideals. He had even sketched out some plans—for he prided himself on his versatility—something white and classic, with a characteristic touch of the baroque, with colonnades where he would walk, discoursing on his aims, and surrounded by an adoring crowd of students.

These dreams had not materialised. The flame of the maestro's enthusiasm had died down to a rather cold ash. The students, though fairly hard working, on the whole, and anxious to learn, had been disappointing. They were always warned that Morosini liked to be called Maestro, but they were always painfully self-conscious in this small matter. They listened to his harangues politely, with unfailing deference, but with an equally unfailing stolidity. Morosini was a naturalised Englishman, and had lived and worked in London for so long that his English was almost perfect, but he could not change his temperament, which was that of a Neapolitan. The school had ceased to amuse him and feed his hungry vanity, and he turned away with a shrug of his shoulders.

"It's still a paying proposition," thought Kent, "but it wouldn't be if he made the damned place weather-proof, and if Hollis and I weren't disgracefully underpaid."

There was a loud crash, followed by a piercing shriek, and Mrs. Pearce came into view at the far end of the passage, running unsteadily towards him. Kent went to meet her.

"What's happened? I say! Hold up!"

She clung to his arm with both hands. "Oh, sir, oh, Mr. Kent, the turn it gave me."

"What is it?"

"In the life room." He could feel her trembling. There was no doubt that she had been profoundly shocked. "The light was on, and it shouldn't have been. And then—I just looked round. Everything seemed as usual, the easels in a semi-circle round the throne—"

"Take your time, Mrs. Pearce. Here, come into the office and sit down, and I'll get you a glass of water."

She shook her head. "No, thanks. I shall be all right—in a minute. It's only," her voice dropped to a whisper, "I never could bear the sight of blood."

"Blood? Where?"

"On the floor, like a strand of dark red wool it was, coming from behind the screen in the corner. Oh, Mr. Kent, I dropped me scuttle!"

"I know," he said. "I heard you. Look here, before we get the wind up, this may be a practical joke. Red paint, you know. Just to get a rise out of you."

"They wouldn't be so cruel to a poor woman that hasn't done them no harm," said Mrs. Pearce pathetically.

"It would be a rotten trick, but they're young, they don't think. Here. Sit down and I'll go and make sure."

Kent had got over his initial alarm and was by now certain that an elaborate booby trap had been set to catch Pearce, who was not a favourite. As he hurried along the corridor he was rehearsing a few scathing remarks that he meant to make presently to the assembled students.

Mrs. Pearce had left the door of the life room open when she fled. The scuttle lay on the threshold, with its contents spilled out on the floor. Kent stepped carefully over the scattered coal and firewood. So far as he could see nothing had been moved since he visited the class the previous afternoon. The easels stood as Mrs. Pearce had described them, fifteen easels bearing fifteen more or less skilful renderings of a golden bobbed head and ivory white flesh. But there was something on the floor in the corner and, as he moved forward he saw what might have been a bundle of clothing in the shadow behind the screen, and, emerging from it, a woman's hand with the fingers splayed out like a starfish.

He went closer to be certain that he was right before he backed away, with a very pale face.

The telephone. Police. For this was a thing that could not be explained away or hushed up because of the harm a scandal would do to the school.

This was murder.

CHAPTER II
WHAT SORT OF ACCIDENT?

The students, arriving towards nine o'clock, found the school gate closed and a notice pinned to the palings.

There has been an accident, and all classes for to-day are cancelled. It is hoped that the school may reopen to-morrow. Please disperse quietly.

The growing crowd milling round the gate paid very little attention to this final admonition.

"What sort of accident? It can't be a fire. There's no smell of burning."

"Perhaps something has happened to Morosini."

"What difference would that make to the work of the school?"

"It's a darned nuisance anyway. My canvas is tacky enough as it is."

"Where's Pearce? We'll make him tell us. Hi! Pearce—" Several joined in. "We want Pearce. We want Pearce—" led by a red-haired girl in magenta trousers and a blue pullover. But the cheerful clamour died down abruptly as the door of the caretaker's cottage opened and the local constable came out.

"Now then, that's quite enough of that. You've read the notice, haven't you? You've all gotta holiday. Ain't that good enough? Don't hang about, blocking up the road. 'Op it, see?"

"Yes, but Binny, darling," said the red-haired girl persuasively, "we want to know what's up. Be a lamb and tell us—or just tell me. You can whisper in my ear."

Police Constable Binns grinned. "No, miss. You go for a nice ride in that motor of yours, but don't let me catch you driving without a light again or you'll get more than a warning."

"All right, but you might tell us."

"You'll hear all about it soon enough. Just you move along now."

The red-haired girl made a face at him, but the hatless youth standing beside her took her arm. "He's right, Gertie, my sweet, a holiday's a lovely thing, God wot, and never mind why. Come along and we'll make the most of it."

They moved away together and the rest followed.

Binns looked after them complacently. He flattered himself that he knew how to manage the students, most of whom had lodgings in the village. A bit loose like in their ways like all these here artists, but no real harm in them. They brought money to the place, and as to goings on—Binns chuckled—there'd been goings on before Mr. Morosini's time, and always would be. He was waiting now for his superiors, not having many ideas of his own on the subject of murder, and he was quite unaware that he had already made one great and irretrievable mistake.

"I don't want to go home," said Betty Haydon to Cherry Garth. "It's the day Auntie has people in to roll bandages. The house will be full of ghastly old pussies."

"We might catch the eleven o'clock bus in to Scan-bridge, have a look at the shops, lunch at the Cadena, and go to the Pictures," suggested Cherry.

"All right. But I bar the Cadena. I've got my sand-wiches."

"So have I. We'll eat them on a seat in the park and get a cup of coffee somewhere."

"What will we do while we wait for the bus? I'm cold already, standing about."

"Mrs. Meggott might make us some tea. Her place is poky, but Prue's Parlour will be full of swanking lifers. I saw Antony and Cleopatra go in there with their crowd."

Cherry and Betty had nicknames for most of their fellow students, and were quite unaware that they them-selves were generally referred to as the mice. Newcomers to Morosini's were usually ignored during their first two or three terms. It was one of the traditions of the school. The friendship between the two latest victims was founded partly on the fact that Betty came by train and Cherry's lodgings were a mile out of the village on the road to the station, and partly because there was nobody else to talk to. Their isolation was embittered for Betty by the know-ledge that there had been exceptions to the rule. If you were very pretty or had charm or—or whatever it was—the men students started talking to you at once. She some-times felt annoyed with Cherry because Cherry did not care. Betty was small and dark, with sharp eyes, in spite of the short sight that obliged her to wear spectacles, and a sharp tongue. Cherry was fair and inclined to be plump, and of a placid and yielding disposition.

Mrs. Meggott, whose picturesque though insani-tary cottage displayed a notice about the sale of tea and minerals, made them welcome, and provided cups of cocoa and slabs of grocer's cake. From her window they saw a police car and an ambulance come up the village street.

Mrs. Meggott, peering out with them, was deeply interested. "Something wrong up at the school, miss? I was wondering how you come to be out at this hour. What is it, if I may ask?"

"We don't know. Binns was there and he shooed us all off."

"There's nobody there at night but the caretaker and his wife," said Betty thoughtfully. "Do you think he can have done her in? He was shell-shocked or something, wasn't he? Everyone says he has a beast of a temper."

"Oh dear, I hope not," said Mrs. Meggott.

"I wonder when it happened," said Cherry. "Everybody had left when we came away yesterday afternoon. You were the last, Betty, you had to go back for your scarf, and I walked on slowly down the hill."

"So I did." Betty finished her cocoa. "Golly. I might be a key witness. What a lark." Her eyes sparkled and a little colour came into her sallow little face at the thought of the attention that might be centred on her.

Mrs. Meggott and Cherry gazed at her with flattering interest.

"Did you see anything, Betty? Oh, do say—"

"My lips are sealed."

Cherry giggled. "I see now. She was having us on, Mrs. Meggott."

"No, I wasn't. But it might not mean anything. I'm not going to talk until I know a lot more than we do now. Cherry, if I give you fivepence you can pay for us both. Come on, or we shall miss the bus. I've just remembered there's an Astaire film at the Corona."

John Kent, meanwhile, after an abortive effort to get in touch with Morosini, had hung up the receiver and resigned himself to wait for the police reinforcements that were coming from Scanbridge. He would have coped with the students as they arrived but Binns had discouraged the idea.

"You stay in this here office, Mr. Kent, and talk to the Inspector when he comes."

Kent occupied the time of waiting in checking up some of the stores of artists' materials kept and dispensed by Miss Roland.

He was burrowing at the back of a drawer for an elusive packet of drawing pins when the door was opened.

"You in charge here?"

The two men who had entered were so large that the tiny office could hardly hold them. The elder of the two had a broad red face with the choleric eye and the small waxed moustache of the typical sergeant major, and Kent took an instant dislike to him. His sleeve brushed a paperweight off the desk as he moved forward, and his companion, who was sandy haired, stooped to pick it up.

"Not exactly. I'm the junior master. But Mr. Hollis isn't here to-day."

"I understand that you found the body?"

"Well—Mrs. Pearce did that. I heard her scream, and then she came and told me. I—I didn't touch anything," said Kent, beginning to feel guilty. "I rang up the police station and Binns was here within ten minutes."

The Inspector grunted. "You'd better come along with us now and show us the place."

"Oh, must I?" said Kent, disliking the idea, and then, realising that his reluctance was regarded as highly suspicious, he rose hastily and led the way along the corridor. He became suddenly voluble, out of sheer nervousness.

"It's a rotten thing to happen and it gave me a most frightful shock. I mean—it's so completely—" his voice died away. He thought, "I'm making an ass of myself. The less I say the better." He stood by while the Inspector unlocked the life room with the key that Binns had given him, and waited in the doorway while the other two went in, after switching on the light.

The Inspector disappeared behind the screen and was there some time while his satellite stood and stared about him at the canvases pinned to the pitch pine walls, and the dark blue curtain blind that was drawn by pulleys across the skylight.

The Inspector emerged from his retirement. His high colour had not faded, but he looked grave.

"Who was this young woman, Mr. Kent?"

"Well, I—I suppose it's Althea. I suppose it must be."

"Why should you feel any doubt?"

"Well," stammered Kent, "I didn't actually see her face, and two or three of the girl students have hair that colour. I mean peroxide."

The Inspector glanced at the paintings on the easels and averted his eyes rather hastily. "She was what you call a model?"

"Yes."

"She's not a local woman?"

The Inspector's tone indicated that he would have liked to add "I hope."

"No. Of course not. She was a professional, and very much sought after at one time. She's getting on now, a bit too old for camera studies. But we were lucky to get her, I thought."

"What was her name?"

"Althea Greville. It's probably a nom de guerre. It's a bit too decorative to ring true, isn't it? However—"

"And her address?"

"I'll have to look it up. We have a list of models in the office. I believe it's somewhere in the Victoria district. Probably a bed-sitting-room. She was down on her luck or she wouldn't have come to us."

"Really? How is that?"

"Oh well, it's a tiresome little train journey for one thing."

"Who engages the models?"

"I do as a matter of fact."

"Not Mr. Morosini?"

"Oh no."

"You knew her well?"

"Good Lord, no. I came across her last year at a party in the studio of a man I know, we got talking and she agreed to sit for the life class here for a fortnight. That was about a year ago. Just lately I ran across her in Town and booked her again. I say—could it have been suicide?

The Inspector answered curtly, "Can't say until we've had the medical report. The doctor'll be here any minute now. You stay here and wait for the others, Owen. Tell them I want pictures from every angle, but Chapman must go over the place first for prints, paying special attention to the wooden frame of the screen. We might get something there. It looks as if it had been knocked over and set up again. You'd better come back with me to the office, Mr. Kent."

In the office the Inspector stationed himself by the window to watch for the doctor's car, and Kent, after lighting another cigarette, perched himself on the edge of the desk, noting as he did so that his companion's broad back blocked out most of the light. He thought, "What a hole this is. No wonder we can't keep a secretary. We seem to be wasting time. I don't believe he knows what to do next. Probably this is his first murder case."

"When did you last see Miss Greville alive, Mr. Kent?"

"Yesterday afternoon, about three o'clock. I went into the life to look at the students' work. One of the girls who has just been promoted from the Prelim was making rather heavy weather of it and I showed her where she was going wrong. I was there about twenty minutes. I didn't speak to the model. There was no occasion."

"I see. And what did you do then?"

"I had already visited the Prelim. I went back to my own studio. I'm doing some illustrations for a firm of publishers. I worked there until the light began to fail and then I went home."

"Is your studio in this building?"

"Yes. It's just along the corridor. Hollis has one, too."

"How is it Mr. Hollis isn't here to-day?"

"He usually takes Thursday off. I have Tuesday. There's nothing official about it. It's just a mutual arrangement."

"Very nice, I daresay," said the Inspector dryly. His manner made it increasingly clear that there was a great deal about the school of which he did not approve. "It all seems very casual. Whose business is it to see that the students don't leave before their time?"

"Nobody's. They aren't children. The youngest is eighteen, and one or two, I believe, are over thirty. They may play about, but they work, too. The model sits from ten to half-past twelve, with a ten-minute break, and then again from two to four-thirty, with a quarter of an hour at half-past three, when she has a cup of tea."

"Who prepares that?"

"The girls have a gas ring in their cloakroom and take turns to see about it."

"Then at half-past four they get their outdoor things and go their ways? No check at all?"

"Precisely."

"No record of attendances?"

"Oh yes. We don't encourage slackers here. They have to sign their names in a book when they arrive in the morning, and the time. The book should be here somewhere. It's the secretary's pidgin." He pulled open a drawer. "Yes, this is it."

"I'll borrow that, if you please, Mr. Kent."

"Certainly."

"How many students are there?"

"Forty-five this term."

"And were they all present yesterday?"

"I believe so."

The Inspector sighed and pulled at his lower lip. The more he learned about this case the less he liked it. "No one sleeps on the premises?"

"No. The caretaker and his wife live in the cottage by the entrance gate."

"Whose job is it to see that the doors are locked at night?"

"Pearce, I suppose. He or his wife always lock the main entrance door, but there are three others. One at the side into the furnace room. There isn't any central heating actually, but the coal is kept there, and one leading to the field at the back where there is a tennis court of sorts, and another that is only used by Mr. Morosini. A path leads from it to a gate into his grounds. I wouldn't like to swear that they are locked every night. Miss Roland keeps change for a couple of pounds in her cash box and she locks the office door and hides the key under the mat, but there's nothing about the place of any value."

"Liberty Hall," said the Inspector sourly. "Anyone could walk in or out. Who cares? But it don't help us much now, Mr. Kent, and that's a fact."

He swung round again to the window as two cars came up, one close behind the other, and his heavy face lit up.

"That's Major Payne, our Chief Constable. I was rather hoping he'd turn up. Just you stay here, Mr. Kent."

He hurried out to meet the newcomers.

Kent flicked his lighter on, and flicked it off again as he realised that he had no more cigarettes left in his case. As he approached the window he saw the ambulance drawn up before the main entrance with two stolid policemen standing by. He turned away quickly, and heard voices in the corridor.

"I think the Superintendent would agree, sir . . . so much on our hands at present . . . I've my own ideas, but proof . . . yes, sir. . . ."

". . . Scotland Yard. . . ."

CHAPTER III
FIFTY SUSPECTS

AT LEAST they haven't waited for the scent to get cold before calling us in," said Collier. "Do you know Scanbridge, Duffield?"

The sergeant, a large, slow man, shook his head. "I looked it up before we left the Yard, when I heard we were being sent down there. A small but prosperous market and manufacturing town on the river Scan, with remains of a Norman castle and Tudor almshouses still occupied by ten old women, within eight miles of the interesting old town of Scanminster, with famous Abbey church. Forty minutes' run from London and an excellent train service."

Collier, who had been looking out at the rather featureless landscape of ploughed fields and pasture under a leaden sky, glanced round with a smile. "What a memory!

Oh, I see. You took notes. Any decent pub where we can put up to-night?"

"There's a trust house," said Duffield hopefully. "Good. And here we are, I fancy."

A car had been sent to meet them, and within a quarter of an hour they were being shown into the Superintendent's room at the police station and introduced to Major Payne, the Chief Constable. The Major shook hands with them both. Collier was relieved to notice that everyone seemed glad to see them. It sometimes happened that Scotland Yard was called in over the heads of local men who had been certain that they needed no extraneous assistance. Collier could be very tactful if he had to be, but that sort of thing added to one's worries. He was a young-looking man, with a slight, active figure, and a lean, clear-cut face that never quite lost its tan during the winter months. His voice was quiet, and he had a friendly and rather deprecating manner which sometimes misled evil-doers into underestimating his abilities.

He listened without interrupting to Inspector Pearson's account of what he had done during the day, only making a few notes. When he had done he said, "According to the doctor the woman had been dead for at least twelve hours and probably more than that?"

"Yes. He says the warmth of the room would delay some of the post-mortem symptoms."

"She was partly dressed. That looks as if she might have been attacked soon after the class was over, while she was getting ready to leave. Has he finished the p.m.?"

"He's doing it now. We're expecting his report any minute."

"I'd like to see her before we go on to the school. Have you taken her finger-prints?"

"No."

"Will you have that done, please, and send them up to the Yard?"

Pearson's florid face had turned a deeper shade of red as he said gruffly that he had thought of it, but he had not had much time.

"We know nothing about her here," said the Chief Constable. "In fact, Mr. Collier, I don't regard this as a local crime. Mr. Morosini and his school are importations. He built himself a house at Parfield some years ago, on the outskirts of the village, and then he bought an adjoining field and put up some deplorably ramshackle buildings and started with only a few students. The villagers gain financially by letting lodgings to these young people, but I happen to know that the neighbouring landowners have always resented what they regard as an intrusion. Between ourselves, the fellow may be a genius and all that, but he's a bounder. And there are subversive elements among the students; only last winter some of them distributed some very mischievous leaflets about what they call blood sports."

"For or against, sir?"

"Oh, against. The young fools. However, we must be fair. There's been no serious law-breaking so far. Those who run cars get pulled in for minor offences, but that's normal. Still, what I say is you never can tell."

Collier suppressed a smile. The Chief Constable was evidently a diehard, but actually, the information he had just imparted might prove useful. He glanced at his notes. "Forty-five students, two masters and a secretary and a caretaker and his wife, any one of whom might be about the place at the time the murder was committed without attracting any particular attention. It's a formidable list of suspects. And it may be her assailant followed her down from London. Well, we can but do our best."

A raw-boned young man with red hair and freckles came in and was introduced as Doctor Anderson, the police surgeon.

"You've done the job?"

"Aye. Here's my report, but I can sum up for ye. Age about thirty-five. Two false teeth in the upper jaw and three stopped in the lower. Man, she must have been a beauty once, and she was still a looker. Her hair was dyed that silly canary colour. It was dark at the roots. Hands well cared for, with the usual horrible red painted nails. Body undernourished, but that proves nothing, as most women are nowadays. No organic disease, but signs of incipient liver trouble due to alcoholism. Injuries, a bruise on the right temple caused by a blow from our dear old friend the blunt instrument, which knocked her out for the moment but wouldn't have been really serious. But the blighter then went on to make a mess of her throat with something sharp."

"A mess?" said Collier.

"Well, no, as a matter of fact, it was quite a neat and efficient incision."

"I see. Thank you." It was evident that most of his hearers thought Anderson's flippancy ill-timed, but Collier, who had a large experience of police doctors, was not sure that he did not prefer it to the more conventional pose of professional dignity.

"Anything else?"

"The time of death? Can you help us there?"

"I'd say it was about four hours after taking her last meal. Make what you can of that. Four or five hours. I'll be going back to folks I can still do some good to now."

He clumped out.

Major Payne frowned. "No manners, but he's said to be very clever."

"That's the main thing," said Collier, who knew that if worldly success was the goal, it wasn't. "I think we'd better see her before we go on to the school."

The Major stood up. "Right. Then I'll be getting along. Ask for anything you want. Anything we can do," he said largely.

"Thank you, sir."

The mortuary was on the other side of the yard. There was the inevitable dripping tap, the smell of carbolic and damp cement, and the usual deathly chill. They came out after ten minutes, not much wiser. Neither Collier nor Duffield had recognised the dead woman. That had been possible, but not likely. The life of an artist's model is too much like hard work to appeal to the criminal classes. The clothing told them little. The cheap art silk underwear was fairly new and bore no laundry marks. The red handbag of imitation leather contained a lipstick and compact, a pocket comb, and a handkerchief heavily scented. A small bottle with three aspirin tablets, a purse with about thirty shillings in silver and copper and a latch key and a few printed cards with the dead woman's name and address.

Miss Althea Greville
17, Bulling Street
Victoria S.W.1.

In one pocket of the bag, behind the mirror, there was a small snapshot, faded and yellow with age, of a young man and woman in bathing suits, sitting on the sands. They had been taken against the light, and both faces were in deep shadow and unrecognisable, but they seemed to be laughing.

"We might have this enlarged," said Collier, "but I don't suppose it's any use."

They found the Superintendent and Pearson waiting for them, expectantly.

"You can't place her?"

Collier shook his head.

"About the inquest. The coroner suggests the day after to-morrow at nine, in the Town Hall. Would that suit you?"

"Yes. We ought to be able to get her landlady to identify her, and then I shall want an adjournment."

"Unless something breaks—"

"As you say," agreed Collier, but he did not sound hopeful. The Superintendent offered a police car and a driver to take them along to the school, and did not conceal his relief when the offer was declined. "The fact is, we're short of everything. These army chaps can rush round in their lorries," he said sourly, "but we have to be careful. There's a good bus service, ten minutes past the hour from Market Square."

Collier looked at his watch. "We can just do it."

He was thinking that it was lucky they had lunched in the train on sandwiches and fruit bought from a station trolley before they started. No offers of refreshment had been made, and, in any case, he grudged time spent on meals at the beginning of an enquiry. Duffield, who had a hearty appetite and would have sat down very willingly to the farmer's ordinary at the King's Head, looked unhappy but resigned.

Pearson had left one of his men at the school gate to take the place of Binns. He was a pleasant-mannered, rosy-cheeked young man, and he gazed at the two men from the Yard with evident awe.

"Anything to report?"

"Nothing, sir. Nobody's been near the place since the body was removed in the ambulance, except a baker with a loaf for the Pearces. Pearce is in bed with one of his bad turns, and his wife is looking after him."

Collier nodded. "I'll have a word with her before we go on to the school."

He knocked at the cottage door, and, after an interval, it was opened by a small, drab, middle-aged woman, who showed them into a tiny, overcrowded parlour smelling of must and mothballs. Her visitors would have preferred the kitchen across the passage where a bright fire was burning.

"Please sit down," said Mrs. Pearce timidly. "You won't mind if I leave the door ajar. I have to listen for Tom."

"I am sorry your husband is ill."

"It's his chest partly, but he gets rheumatism too this time of year."

"Does it come on suddenly?"

"Not really, but he keeps about as long as he can."

"When did he take to his bed this time?"

She kept her work-worn hands clasped in her lap. He saw the knuckles whiten as she answered.

"I went into Scanbridge to do my week's shopping yesterday, and when I come home I found him sitting by the kitchen fire doubled up with pain, so I helped him upstairs and hotted a bottle and gave him a nice strong cup of tea after a dose of his new medicine, and he went off like a lamb. And—and"—she went on with a rush—"round about seven I remembered the school, so I took the key and went off and locked the front door, but I never went inside nor nothing. How was I to know there'd be something amiss that night of all nights?"

"You couldn't know, of course," said Collier soothingly. "Your husband follows a routine, I suppose? I mean, he goes into all the rooms and attends to the stoves and so forth."

"Not the stoves. They're not the sort that keep in all night, worse luck. But he does look to make sure the lights haven't been left on anywhere."

"There are three other doors besides the main one. He would look to those?"

"Yes, sir. But there's only the one to the tennis court that the students use to run in and out. The other's only open when we get in coal, and Mr. Morosini's way in is never used by anybody else."

"The garden door was not locked when Inspector Pearson tried it this morning."

Mrs. Pearce swallowed hard. "I'm very sorry, sir," she said humbly. "I'm the one to blame for that. What with Tom being so poorly, and the black-out—do you—do you think the murderer came and went that way, sir?"

"I can't say about that yet. But don't worry. You were quite right to be frank with me."

"If Mr. Morosini sacks my husband for this I don't know where we shall go."

"I hope he won't," said Collier. He could not say more than that.

Whatever the reason the Pearces were to some extent responsible. He reflected a moment and glanced at his sergeant, who was unobtrusively taking notes of their conversation. "What time did you get home yesterday?"

"I caught the ten-past four, so it would be a little before five. I was that flustered seeing Tom so bad that I just set down my parcels—"

"Everyone would be out of the school by then?"

"Yes. Although Mr. Kent sometimes stayed on, busy with his own work. Mr. Hollis never does, because his wife likes him to be punctual. She's a terror, they say. I know because a niece of mine was parlour-maid there once. Mind you, it's a lovely house, and everything just so, and before the war they used to go abroad for their holidays and stay at the best hotels. But it's her money, and he's only got what he earns."

"Is Mr. Kent married?"

"Not him. He lives with his sister. They call the house Poona. It's just down the lane on your left."

"He was at the school this morning when you found the body?"

"Yes, sir. Luckily. I don't know what I should have done if I'd been alone."

"Does he usually arrive as early as that?"

"Well, no, he doesn't. But he said he was expecting a letter."

"Would his letters be addressed to the school?"

"Not as a general thing, they wouldn't. But there's no law against it. I thought to myself maybe it was something he didn't want his sister to know about. Always pushing her nose in, she is. The vicar's right hand. Right hand, my foot. It's just interferingness. But as for taking good care of the poor man, tinned food and something cold in the larder when he gets in; and holes in his socks."

"I see. About Miss Greville now. Was she one of the regular models?"

"No. She was here for about three weeks last year. In June, it was. We don't have her sort as a rule. You mightn't think it, sir, but most of them are decent, well-behaved young women, and you wouldn't know when they had their clothes on that they ever took them off, in a manner of speaking."

"Wasn't she well-behaved?"

Little Mrs. Pearce looked down her nose. "I couldn't say about that. I saw very little of her, and she wasn't one to pass the time of day with anyone like me. Why men go wild about that sort passes me, but there it is."

"Did she make trouble here?"

"Not to my knowledge, sir."

Collier glanced at Duffield and they both stood up. "Thank you again, Mrs. Pearce. I hope your husband will soon be better. I'd like a few words with him."

"He's got a temperature," she said quickly. "He's not fit to see anybody at present."

"I wonder what she's so frightened about," said Duffield when they had left the caretaker's cottage and were walking up the drive to the school buildings.

"That's obvious. She either knows her Tom committed the murder, or she is afraid he may have done. There would have been time before she came in from her shopping expedition."

"Yes. He could have," said Duffield, who needed time himself to catch up mentally with his superior officer. "But why?"

"We shall have to look into that. I don't think it's very likely. Just one of the possibilities we'll have to bear in mind."

"She didn't mind spilling the beans about other people."

"Very voluble," Collier agreed. "A sign of nervous strain." He fitted the key into the lock of the main door. "If there is a place more dreary than an empty theatre it's an empty school." They looked into the secretary's office, into the preliminary classroom, where plaster casts loomed ghostly in the gathering dusk. A stick of charcoal crunched under Collier's foot as he moved forward. There were several canvases leaning against the walls. All represented the same subject, the head and shoulders of a grey-bearded old man wearing a blue and red checked muffler. Back in the corridor, Collier consulted the plan of the school buildings that Pearson had given him.

"The adjoining room is unused at present. Then come the private rooms of the two masters—"

They looked into the cupboard in which the caretaker kept his brooms and brushes, noting that there was room in it for a man to stand upright. Mr. Kent's room was that of a worker, his table littered with sketches, and a nearly finished drawing in ink and wash pinned to a board. A crumpled and paint-smeared overall hung over the back of his chair. The floor under the table was strewn with cigarette ends. Collier switched on his torch and picked up several stubs. He showed Duffield a red stain on one stub.

"Lipstick. I'll keep these. We must find out how often these rooms are cleaned. By the look of things not more than once a week." The room of the senior master presented a complete contrast. There was no sign of any work on hand, a shabby but comfortable wicker chair had been left drawn up to the gas fire, and within reach there was a shelf well stocked with detective fiction and travel books. An old envelope had been left in one of the novels as a marker. Collier opened the book to look at it. The envelope was blank, but the back had been covered with tiny sketches in profile of a woman's face. Collier examined them carefully before he asked Duffield's opinion.

"Who is this, would you say?"

"It's her," said Duffield after a moment. "I noticed her nose. A short straight nose with rather wide nostrils, and the rather heavy brows, unusual these days when so many women have them plucked."

"You mean—Althea Greville." He returned the envelope to the book, one of the earlier novels of Lynn Brock, and replaced it carefully on the shelf. "I thought so too. Unfortunately it does not prove anything. According to Mrs. Pearce, who loathed her, she mowed them down in swathes. Let's get on. I want to see all the rooms before the light fails."

He spent a comparatively short time in the life class-room.

"Nothing for us here. Pearson and his lads seem to have gone over it thoroughly, photographs, measurements, fingerprints."

Duffield moved about looking at the students' work on the easels. Collier glanced at his wooden face and suppressed a smile.

"What do you think of them?"

"I don't know much about art," said Duffield, with his usual caution.

The cloak-rooms for the men and the women students were dark and dingy. In each there were overalls hanging on a row of hooks, and a small spotted looking-glass of the quality that can be bought for sixpence at a multiple store nailed to the pitch-pine partition, and in each there were four washbasins and taps and a roller towel behind the door.

"Very primitive arrangements here," said Duffield disapprovingly.

Collier agreed. "A moribund concern. Don't touch the taps. Have you the insufflator? Good. This may be where the local people slipped up. They don't seem to have bothered about the usual offices, and it's just possible that the murderer washed his hands before he left."

"He might," said Duffield, as he prepared to puff yellow powder over the surfaces indicated by his superior officer. "But this won't help us unless he's a stranger. A whole lot of people have a perfect right to paw round here."

"Fifty suspects," sighed Collier, "and from all we have heard so far the deceased wasn't a very valuable member of society."

"We haven't heard her side," Duffield reminded him.

"Poor creature. You're right. How long will you be over this job?"

"Another half-hour."

"Very well. You may as well take the films back to the Yard to be developed. I want you to go back to Town to-night anyway. Go to Bulling Street and find out as much as you can about Miss Greville. I may spend the night in the village if I can get a bed at the inn. If not I shall put up at the King's Head in Scanbridge. Ring me up at the Scanbridge police station to-morrow morning about nine."

"Very good, sir."

CHAPTER IV
THE END OF THE FIRST DAY

THE village itself was undoubtedly picturesque in Ye Olde tradition, but building developments had spoilt its outskirts in the Edwardian period when a golf course had been opened a few miles away and cheaper cars had made it possible for the business man to move farther out of London. But the course, for some reason, had never become popular, and for some years now fields that had been hopefully described as eligible sites had lain fallow.

Collier stopped at the Green Man on his way up the village street and booked a room for the night. He then asked to be directed to Mr. Kent's house, and the landlord came out with him to point the way.

"You mean Mrs. Mansfield's place. Another hundred yards and turn down a lane on your left. You can't mistake it as it stands alone. Mr. Kent used to lodge with us, and the wife and I did our best to make him comfortable, but Mrs. Mansfield came home from India when her husband died, and she took that house and moved in her furniture that was in store and told us Mr. Kent would be living with her in future. He was away on his holidays at the time, and it's my opinion he knew nothing at all about it, but of course he had to fall in with her wishes, she being his sister and so much older than him, and left a widow and all—"

"The first on the left, you said?"

"Yes, sir."

Collier reflected that both the staff masters at Morosini's appeared to be more or less under some woman's thumb. It was a fact that probably had no bearing on the case, but he was still at the stage of picking up pieces. In his experience scraps of apparently irrelevant information had sometimes proved vital.

He went some fifty yards down a miry lane between high, unkempt hedges of hazel and alder before he reached his destination. It was still just light enough for him to see the name on the gate. Poona. The front garden looked dank and neglected and an overhanging branch of laurel gave him an unexpected showerbath as he passed under it. He rang the bell, and the door was opened after an interval, by a youngish man in grey flannel slacks and a green sports coat.

"I'm afraid Mrs. Mansfield is out."

"I wanted to see Mr. Kent."

"That's all right then. That's me. Will you come in?" He led the way into a shabby dining-room. On the table there were remains of a solitary and not very appetising meal.

"Wait a minute. I'll just draw the curtains. Do please sit down." He poked the fire. "We may as well be comfortable," he remarked, "and now, what can I do for you?"

Though his manner was friendly and genial he looked tired and worried and Collier noticed that his hand shook as he held out his cigarette case.

Collier introduced himself and added that he was hoping that Mr. Kent would be able to help him.

"I will if I can, of course. But oughtn't you to warn me, or something? I mean, the local police seemed to think—"

"I don't suspect anyone at present, Mr. Kent. I hope you will answer questions, but you need not if you don't want to," said Collier, smiling. "I have seen the statement you made this morning to Inspector Pearson and I don't want to waste your time and my own by covering the same ground. Would you say that Miss Greville had a very striking, an unusual personality?"

"Yes. I suppose you might call it that. That is, she wasn't clever, so far as I know. I never heard her make any but the most ordinary remarks, and she had rather a common voice. But she couldn't come into a crowded room without attracting attention. You found yourself watching her. There was a definite reason for that from an artist's point of view. She was the most graceful woman I have ever seen, her every movement was—I don't know how to describe it—fluid. It's a physical quality rare in the Anglo-Saxon race. You get it more often in the Latin countries, and, of course, with Indians."

"That would make her an exceptionally good model?"

"Yes, and I believe that years ago she worked for some of the big pots. But she had her drawbacks. My friend, at whose studio I met her last year, told me that in her palmy days she was very temperamental and capricious and couldn't be trusted not to let you down by walking out when your picture was only half finished. But there had been a fairly long period during which nothing had been heard of her, and she had turned up looking much older and not nearly so prosperous, and, apparently, in a very chastened frame of mind. I sounded her about coming down here to pose for our students and she agreed. I engaged her for three weeks. Her poses were quite different to the usual well-worn stances and our students were very bucked and the work, I remember, was well above the normal rather depressing level of mediocrity."

"How is it that you waited more than a year before engaging her again?"

Kent hesitated. "Well—so far as I know she was on her best behaviour while she was here. I was busy at the time with some illustrating work, and I hardly saw her outside the class. But I suppose I felt that she was potentially dangerous."

"Dangerous? In what way exactly?"

"I didn't reason it out. You get that feeling about some people, I suppose. There had been stories about her. One of the fellows she used to sit for shot himself. No one knew why, and it might not have been anything to do with her. I think—I think myself that if she chose to try she could get any man, not for keeps, of course, but long enough to ruin him."

"Events seem to have proved you right, Mr. Kent."

Kent groaned. "Don't rub it in. I shall never cease to regret that we had her back. But the model who was to have come failed us and I had just had a letter from Miss Greville asking if we could give her some work and saying that she was down and out. I never liked her, but I was sorry—"

"How long has she been here this time?"

"Since last Monday week."

"Doesn't Mr. Morosini take any part in running this school?"

"He pays us an occasional visit, and he picks out what he considers the best work done in the preliminary class at the end of each term and decides who is to be promoted to the life class, but he is often away painting portraits. He spent some months in the States last year. Bello Sguardo is his headquarters when he is at home, though he has a studio and a flat in Town."

"Is he at home now?"

"I shouldn't know. He has not been in the school this term but he may look in any time. There are rumours that he is going to be married to one of his sitters. His portrait of her was in last year's Academy."

"Anyone particular?"

"Oh dear, yes. Lady Violet Easedal, only daughter of some Earl, or perhaps he's a Marquis. A very posh connection."

"I see. Just between ourselves, is Mr. Morosini a social climber?"

Kent grinned. "And how!"

"He hasn't spent much on the school lately."

"He's tired of it. But it has been a paying proposition. This isn't going to do it any good. The wrong kind of publicity."

"I'm afraid so," said Collier. "You don't like him, do you?"

"Not much, I'm afraid," Kent admitted, "but you mustn't pay any attention to my ebullitions of spite. I'm a darned failure—just a hard-working hack—and he's so blatant. I see myself as time passes getting more and more like that poisonous fellow in *Troilus and Cressida*, what was his name—Thersites."

"You can say what you like to me," said Collier comfortably. "There used to be an A.C. at the Yard got my goat in the same way."

"Actually," said Kent, "the job I have at the school suits me. I should be sorry to lose it. I have to help my sister who was left a widow with two children to start in life. And that reminds me, Inspector. Can we re-open as usual to-morrow?"

"Certainly. I think I must keep the classroom in which the murder was committed shut up for the present, but I noticed you had another room not in present use."

"Yes. Our numbers have gone down in the last four or five years."

"Another point. I should like to say a few words to the students collectively at some time during the morning. Could you arrange that?"

"No difficulty about that. They'll be delighted," said Kent.

"Anything else?"

"I don't think so," said Collier casually, as he got up to go. "Oh, about the other master—I understand he is away on holiday?"

"Oh no. He usually has Thursday off. The Hollises have a car and they may have gone up to Town for lunch and a matinée. They wouldn't hear about our trouble until they came home unless there's a lot about it in the evening papers."

"There won't be. About to-morrow. Would ten suit you?"

Kent nodded. "I'll have them ready for you." He went with Collier to the door. It was quite dark by now and Collier switched on his torch. As he walked down the drive two people were coming down the lane. He heard the high, petulant voice of a young man and an older woman replying. "My dear boy, what does it matter who loses when we aren't playing together?"

"Does that mean that you're going to hand over fifty per cent of your winnings?"

"It does not. You're always borrowing and never pay back."

"Well, of all the damned—" the young man broke off abruptly as he became aware of a shadowy figure holding the gate open for them to pass in. The dimmed light of a torch moved over them both and went out. He said sharply "Who is it?"

"Sorry," said Collier, "I didn't mean to dazzle you. This black-out business is a nuisance, isn't it. Good night."

They both stared after him as he vanished into the darkness.

"Darned cheek," grumbled the boy. "What was he doing at our place?"

"It was probably one of the students from the school come to see John about something." She let herself into the house with a latchkey and switched on the light in the passage.

"John, are you there?"

Kent came out of the dining-room. "Hallo, Agatha, I didn't expect you home so early."

"Mrs. Gale and Arnold had rotten luck, and she's a bad loser. She got so cross that I thought we had better come away before she went too far. I hope you've kept up the fire, John. I'm simply frozen after forty minutes in a draughty bus."

Kent followed his sister and her son into the dining-room. Mrs. Mansfield was a stout, hard-faced woman, very smartly turned out, with hennaed hair carefully waved. She was fifteen years older than Kent. Arnold, who was twenty, was a good-looking young man and rather too obviously aware of the fact. He glanced scornfully at the remains of his uncle's meal on the table and murmured, "How sick making."

Agatha Mansfield sank into an easy chair and held out her hands to the blaze. "I needn't have worried about the fire," she said disagreeably. "Trust you to take care of yourself."

Kent lit another cigarette. "Why not? I expect I shall be asked to pay the coal bill."

Mrs. Mansfield's thin red lips tightened. John was usually so uncomplaining that she had got into the habit of venting her ill humour on him. She had never really liked her young half-brother, for she had bitterly resented her father's second marriage, but he had been useful since she returned from India as a widow with an exiguous income and two children to start in life. She had jockeyed him very cleverly into sharing a house with her, and relied on his contributions to the family exchequer, but she gave him as little as possible in return. She was a bad housekeeper, and never kept a maid for long. They were without one at present, but a woman from the village came in for an hour or two every morning.

Arnold, who had not yet found an occupation to his liking, had recently returned home. He had been living in London doing what he had vaguely described as a temporary job. His mother spoiled him and so far he had evaded any attempt by Kent to bring him to book.

Mrs. Mansfield kicked off her shoes and wriggled her toes luxuriously. In the matter of silk stockings, she reflected, it paid to buy the best.

"Who was that man who barged into us at the gate?"

Kent answered briefly, "Police."

Mrs. Mansfield was too well made up to show any change of colour, but she started perceptibly and glanced at Arnold.

"I told you, darling, that if you owed your landlady, or anybody, we would pay. People are so grasping—"

Arnold answered sulkily, "I don't owe anything. It's nothing to do with me. Why must you always pick on me? John's human, too. What was it, John? Riding your push bike to the common danger?"

"It's serious," Kent said. "Murder. Mrs. Pearce found the model's body lying behind the screen in the life class-room this morning. I had just arrived, luckily, and I rang up Binns. The Scanbridge people were on the spot within the hour and they got busy, but apparently they felt the case was too much for them to handle. That fellow who was here just now came from Scotland Yard and I gathered that he was in charge. Quite a decent sort of chap, a distinct improvement on the local cops."

"My dear John," cried his sister, "how ghastly! But do tell us all about it."

She was so full of questions and comments that Kent hardly noticed his nephew's silence.

Collier meanwhile had returned to the main road and went back through the village, keeping close to garden palings and hedges to avoid an occasional motor, until he came to the ornate wrought-iron gates of Bello Sguardo. But here he drew a blank. The sleek Italian manservant who opened the door said that his master was not at home

"I am an inspector of police. I have to get in touch with him. Do you know where he is?"

"I could ring up Park Street, sir. My master has a flat and studio there. But he may be staying with friends. He left no address."

"When did he go up?"

"Last night after dinner."

"That would be about eight o'clock?"

"Yes, sir."

"He went by car?"

"Yes, sir."

"Well, ring up the flat. I'll speak to him if he is there."

"Very good, sir."

The servant opened the door of a sedan chair that stood at the foot of the stairs and closed it after him. Collier followed him and opened it. The man, who had been in the act of picking up the receiver, looked round angrily.

"My master likes this door to be closed when the telephone is being used."

"Does he?" said Collier genially. "I was just admiring the interior fittings. Charming. Quite a museum piece. Carry on, and don't mind me."

He examined the ivory-painted panels with their little wreaths of roses and flying cupids with genuine admiration while making a mental note of the call number and listening to the ensuing conversation.

"Romilda? This is Beppi. There is an inspector of police here who wishes to speak to the padrone. Is he there? No? Where is he? You do not know?"

"Just a minute." Collier took the receiver from him. "Will you tell Mr. Morosini that the police hope he will return at once to Bello Sguardo. They need his assistance. The matter is urgent. Good-bye."

He hung up.

Beppi's black eyes were still angry, but he said nothing.

Collier glanced round the hall at the frescoed walls, the mosaic floor, the gilt lanterns hanging from the ceiling, and the central fountain with its bronze copy of the boy with the dolphin from the Palazzo Pubblico in Florence.

"Quite a nice place you have here," he said pleasantly. He thought of the cracked wash-basins in the school cloakrooms.

Beppi waited implacably by the door to show him out, but Collier still lingered. "You know what happened at the school?"

"I have heard. Yes."

"How did you hear?"

"I went into the village to post a letter. The woman in the post office talked."

"You speak English very well."

"I am English."

"Naturalised, like your master? I see. Have you tried to communicate with Mr. Morosini since you heard of the murder?"

"No, sir. It was all rumour and hearsay. I did not know what to believe. I thought it best to wait."

"Very well. Good night."

Beppi closed the door after him without deigning to reply.

Surly brute, thought Collier, as he trudged down the drive. He always disliked dealing with menservants, holding that their training made them deceitful. He was tired and was looking forward to supper and bed, but he still had one more visit to pay before he could call it a day.

CHAPTER V
MORE LIGHT ON ALTHEA

KENT, turning in at the school gate, nearly collided with Cherry Garth.

"Sorry," he said as he got off his bicycle, "careless of me." He knew her vaguely as one of the newcomers. She seemed very shy. He had never seen her before without her friend, the sallow dark-haired girl with the sharp voice. "Alone to-day?" he said. "Where's Miss What's-her-name?"

"Betty Haydon? She must have missed her train. She comes from Scanminster."

"That's unfortunate. It's rather important that all the students should be here to-day."

"Oh, is it? She'll come later, I expect."

As they walked up the drive together, Cherry's heart was beating faster than usual. She was thinking, "He doesn't know, he never will know, how terribly I care for him. He hardly ever noticed me before to-day."

Kent slouched along by her side, wheeling his bicycle.

"I suppose you've heard what happened here Wednesday evening?"

"My landlady told me this morning that they are saying in the village that the model was—was murdered. I—I didn't really believe it."

"Unfortunately it's the truth. You'll hear all about it. The students are to assemble in the Prelim at ten. I'm just going to put a notice on the board."

"How perfectly awful!" cried Cherry. "Won't it be very bad for the school?"

"I'm afraid it will."

They parted at the door, and she passed entirely out of his mind, but she went on thinking about him. She could not help feeling rather glad that Betty had missed her train. If Betty had been with her she would have been brisk and competent, and she—Cherry—would not have had the courage to utter a word. Betty always took the lead. She was not in the least interested in any of the students or in Mr. Kent, her affections being more or less fixed on Fred Astaire and Robert Taylor, who were a long way off in Hollywood. Sometimes she made fun of Kent and then Cherry pretended to laugh at him too. She did not want Betty to guess her secret.

Students were crowding into the cloakroom as she hung up her hat and coat and buttoned on her overall. They were all talking about the murder.

"My dear, it's ghastly, but it's thrilling, too—"

"I think it's horrible—"

"I wonder why. I mean, who could it have been—"

"She wasn't very young. She had been lovely, of course."

"Did you read all the notices on the board? It must have taken Mr. Kent quite a time to type them out. I must say I'm glad he doesn't expect us to work in the room where it happened. I may be tough, but I'm not as tough as that—"

Cherry slipped away unnoticed, to take her accustomed place in the preliminary classroom. Naturally, as she was a newcomer, it was a place nobody else wanted, in rather a dark corner. There was a draped model; usually an old man or woman from the village, on Mondays, Tuesdays and Wednesdays, but during the remainder of the week the students who had not yet been promoted to drawing from the life made studies in charcoal from plaster casts. Cherry had been put down to the Apollo Belvedere and by this time she had developed a violent dislike for his too perfect profile and his curls.

The other students drifted in and took their places. She overheard scraps of their conversation.

Everyone, of course, was talking about the murder, and envying the life class people for having what might be described as ring-side seats.

"What was this model like? I don't believe I ever saw her—"

"Hot stuff. You know that roadhouse, Swings and Horses, that was closed when the War started? I saw her there once last year with two of the life class chaps, all three of them blotto."

"Who were they?"

"I'm not telling. One of them has left the school anyway. It's ages ago. But it just shows."

Kent had had a short and rather acid colloquy with the school secretary, Miss Roland, over the telephone. She had rung up to inform him that she was not coming back.

"Why not? A week's notice is usual—"

"I'm ever so sorry, but my mother was very upset and so was my fiancée when I told them what had happened. It isn't very nice, Mr. Kent, and a girl must think of herself—"

"Oh, all right—" he hung up.

Collier arrived a few minutes before ten and found Kent waiting for him in the office. Kent apologised for the absence of Mr. Hollis. "He's apt to be late, but he ought to be here any minute."

"I'm afraid not," said Collier. "I thought you might have heard. I called at the house last night. The parlour-maid told me she had just been rung up by Mrs. Hollis. It's very unfortunate. They had lunch and did some shopping and went to a show at the Odeon in Leicester Square. When they came out Mr. Hollis was knocked down as they were crossing the road. They hope his injuries aren't serious, but he was unconscious and had to be taken in an ambulance to a nursing home in Wimpole Street. Mrs. Hollis hopes to bring him home if he can be moved, to-day, but it sounds as if you wouldn't be seeing him at the school for a little while."

"I say, I'm awfully sorry," said Kent. "Poor old Hollis. One is apt to laugh at him, fond of the fleshpots and all that, but he's a good sort in many ways."

"I'll see the students now."

"Very well." Kent led the way to the preliminary classroom and introduced the Inspector. Collier looked over the assembled ranks. He seemed blandly impervious to the concentrated gaze of so many eyes.

"Good morning, ladies and gentlemen. I won't keep you long. I think it would be a good idea to check up on the attendance to begin with. Could we have a roll call, Mr. Kent?"

"Certainly." Kent asked one of the older men students to fetch the attendance book and went rapidly through the names. There were three absentees. Of these two had sent notes to excuse themselves on account of colds. The third was Betty Haydon.

Kent looked across the room and saw the round face of Cherry Garth peeping shyly round her easel.

"What about your friend, Miss—ah—"

"She's probably missed her train," said Cherry, blushing violently at the attention she was attracting. "She comes over from Scanminster. She'll be here later."

"That's all right," said Collier easily, no sixth sense warning him that Betty was important. "Now I expect you have all heard rumours. I am going to tell you the facts. The body of the model who has been posing for the life class was found behind the screen in the life classroom yesterday morning by Mrs. Pearce, when she went in to light the stove. According to the medical evidence, she was probably stunned by a blow on the temple, but the actual cause of death was a stab with some sharp instrument. She was partly dressed and our present theory is that she was attacked soon after the end of the afternoon class while she was getting ready to go home. Now I want your help. I want you all, especially, of course, the members of the life class, to try to remember anything that happened on Wednesday afternoon that might have a bearing on this case. I would like a statement from those who were the last to leave. You may have heard that Mr. Hollis has met with an accident. In his absence I am going to use his room. Please come to me there. And please don't be alarmed or worried by all this. One of my colleagues is coming in now. He wants to take your fingerprints, and I hope you will all agree to having this little operation performed. I can assure you that it is quite painless, and it isn't going to help us very much. It is just a matter of routine." He paused, and resumed in a graver tone. "I want you to conquer any reluctance you may feel about coming to me to tell me any little thing you may have noticed. This was a brutal and a cold-blooded business. I don't want to harrow you, but please don't forget that. Thank you."

He stepped down from the model's throne on which he had stood to deliver his oration, with a sigh of relief, for though he usually got on well enough with the younger generation, he preferred to deal with them singly.

Kent went with him to the door. "Can they get on with their work now?"

"Certainly. But, look here, if nobody volunteers to beard me in my den, they must send in two students to represent the life class, a man and a girl."

"In that order?"

"No. I'll see the girl first." He looked at his watch. "As soon as possible, please. I have an appointment in Scanbridge at twelve."

"I'll tell them." Kent hesitated and then said abruptly, "I don't think they can help you. The crime must have been committed by somebody who followed her here from London."

"We have not overlooked that possibility, Mr. Kent."

It was cold in Mr. Hollis's room and Kent lit the gas fire. "Very neat," he remarked, "compared with my pigsty."

"Mr. Hollis doesn't do any work apart from teaching?"

"No. He used to, but his stuff hadn't much sale, though it was damned good, I thought; and his wife crabbed his work. A chap loses heart, I suppose, and of course he doesn't need the money. I mean, she runs the whole show, and expense is no object. The only thing he has hung on to so far is this teaching job. It gives him some illusion of independence and enables him to pay his tailors' bills."

"Have they been married long?"

"Getting on for two years."

Collier looked after him thoughtfully as he went out. He rather liked John Kent, but he fancied there was more to him than met the eye. He had not been waiting long when the door opened to admit a red-haired girl in a green overall.

"They've sent me. I hope you don't mind?" she said gaily.

"Miss Tressider, isn't it? Won't you sit down?"

"How did you know my name?"

"I heard the roll call."

"Can you place us all after that? You must be pretty marvellous."

He smiled. "I'm afraid not. I just happened to notice you."

"I see." She heaved an exaggerated sigh. "My horrible hair. It makes me so conspicuous."

His smile broadened. "Do I offer my condolences?"

She was looking at him curiously. "I say, you're not a bit like a policeman."

His smile had vanished. "Don't be too sure of that, Miss Tressider. You were present at the afternoon class on Wednesday. Was everything quite normal?"

"I think so. Mr. Kent came in about his usual time, between two and three, and made the round. He worked for about ten minutes on my right knee—I mean, of course, on my painting. I often get my knees woolly somehow."

"When did the model have her rest?"

"From twenty to half-past three. Then she went on until half-past four."

"What do you do exactly when you leave?"

"Bung our paintboxes into our lockers in the passage, and rush for the cloakroom to shed our overalls and put on our outdoor things. Some people clean their brushes with turps and put them away with their boxes, but I always take mine home and wash them in soapy water. I've got a very decent landlady and she lets me have plenty of hot water."

"Were you the last to leave the classroom?"

"Tommy Brock and I came out together. He's coming in to see you next. I hope you won't think we murdered her."

"Where was she when you left the classroom?"

"She had gone behind the screen. I heard her strike a match. She smoked a lot."

"Did you, at any time, have any conversation with her?"

"No. One or two of the girls spoke to her, trying to be friendly and human, but they were badly snubbed. I prefer men to women myself," said Miss Tressider candidly, "but one need not be rude."

"Quite," said Collier, amused. "She let the men talk to her?"

"I wouldn't say that either. I thought she had changed a lot since last year. She was in high spirits then, and I happen to know that several of the boys were quite silly about her, considering she was old enough to be their mother. It was all right to rave about her from one point of view—as a model she was marvellous—but from every other point she let the place down, and a lot of us were very glad when she left and pretty sick when she turned up again last week. But, as I was telling you, she had changed. She seemed down on her luck, and, of course, with the time of year and the black-out there isn't much opportunity for dalliance after working hours."

"I understand that she came to and fro from London on a Green Line coach. Did any of the students go the same way?"

"I don't think so. We practically all live in digs in or near the village. A few come from Scanbridge, but that's a different bus service."

Collier thought a moment. Miss Tressider struck him as being a hard-boiled young woman, but fundamentally an honest and reliable witness. He said, "The Pearce couple, are they generally liked?"

"Mrs. Pearce is a dear, and absolutely straight. He's all right, I suppose, but he was badly wounded and gassed in the last War. He's got a temper, and he's moody at times. A bit of a scrounger like most old soldiers. I mean, he gets more civil towards Christmas time."

"You're being very helpful, Miss Tressider. I wonder if you are prepared to be equally frank about Mr. Morosini himself."

She shrugged her shoulders. "Why not? But I can't give you a close up. He gives an At Home to the students at Bello Sguardo about three times a year. Lemonade and biscuits and weak tea, but the house is gorgeous; and he pays us a flying visit here at least once a term towards the end, to mark our work. Don't misunderstand me. I'm not running him down. He's a genius. His stuff is in the direct line from Velasquez."

"But as a man?"

She shook her head. "I wouldn't know. Really. Nobody knows. His servants are all Italian. I believe he has week-end parties, but we don't know anything about them in the village."

"I see. Well, thank you, anyway. I won't keep you any longer, Miss Tressider."

Tom Brock proved equally willing to talk, but he was not able to add very much to the sum of information Collier had already acquired. Yes, some of the fellows had fallen for Miss Greville. He had not. She was not his type. There was not much in it, so far as he knew, dancing and supper at a road house that had since been closed down, runs up to Town to dine and see a movie.

"That was last year, of course, when she was staying here. It was summer time and the evenings were long and light. Nothing doing this time."

"Who were her special friends, Mr. Brock?"

But this proved to be too direct a question. Tom Brock either could not or would not remember.

Collier thanked him, and hurried off to catch the bus into Scanbridge, where he was to report to the Chief Constable. He hoped Major Payne was not expecting quick results. He had feared from the first that it was not going to be that sort of case.

The Major had arrived just before him and he was. taken directly to the superintendent's room.

Payne greeted him heartily. "Well, Mr. Collier, have you brought good news? The end in sight, eh?"

"I only came in on the case yesterday afternoon, sir. These murders on neutral ground are always difficult."

"What do you mean by neutral ground?"

"A place where neither the murderer nor his victim belongs and where a lot of other people have a right to be, such as a common, a wood, or, in this case, a school. So far I've been collecting possibles. It is quite a long list. The caretaker or his wife, the two staff masters, any one of the fifteen life class students, Mr. Morosini himself. Any one of these could have got in to the building at dusk, when the others had left, and slipped out again unnoticed. We're taking fingerprints, but they won't do much for us. When the students leave this afternoon we shall make sure no overalls are taken away. I'm going to have them all sent up to the Yard to be tested for bloodstains. Sergeant Duffield went back to London last night to handle that end. I went over the school yesterday, and again this morning before anybody else was about. The door opening into the coal shed is sprung and the lock does not catch. Anyone could get in and out that way. I noticed traces of coal dust on the floor in the corridor, but Pearce and his wife go in and out with scuttles filling up the stoves, and Mrs. Pearce told me that the floors are only washed over once a week, on Saturdays."

"If you take my advice, Inspector," said the Major, "you'll look for the motive. It wasn't robbery, obviously. There was nearly thirty shillings in the poor woman's bag. Oh, by the way, have you seen Mr. Morosini yet?"

"Not yet. I hope to do so to-day."

"Just so. But I'd go easy there if I were you. I won't say he is popular here, but he's a person of some importance I believe. I am told that he has been commissioned to paint portraits of members of the Royal Family and that he may get something in the next birthday honours."

"I try not to upset people if I can help it," said Collier with deceptive meekness. He was getting rather tired of Major Payne. Fortunately the Chief Constable had said his say, and he was allowed to go. He was on his way to London where he had arranged to meet Sergeant Duffield, but first he called at the Green Line coach station where he succeeded in interviewing one of the conductors on the coach that left for London at 4.15. Collier described Miss Greville. The conductor remembered her.

"One of these ersatz blondes, but a looker all right. We picked her up several days running lately and always at the same place outside of that school place outside of Elder Green. Yes, I recollect her red handbag. Haven't seen her the last day or two. No, she never had nobody with her. Kept herself to herself more than most of her sort."

Duffield was waiting by the bookstall in Victoria Station, and the two men had a hurried snack in the refreshment room while the sergeant made his report.

"I've seen her landlady. A Mrs. Corbin. Hard as nails. Believe me, she didn't bat an eyelid when I told her what had happened to her tenant. At least, I called it a fatal accident. But it seems Miss Greville only moved in a month ago. The house is let out in so-called flatlets at a weekly rent. That means a bed sitter with a gas ring. I will say Mrs. C. keeps the passage and the stairs clean, and apparently she insists on a fairly high moral standard. I gathered that she made a distinction between the steady boy friend and the casual pick up, the latter not being allowed. She said that Miss Greville had no references, but paid a week in advance, and that she had no reason to complain of her behaviour. She said she fancied Miss Greville drank pretty heavily. She was away all day during the week, but spent her Sundays in bed with a whisky bottle within reach. She didn't make friends with anyone and never spoke when you passed her on the stairs. Not matey by any means."

"You went through her room?"

"Yes. She had very little more than what she stood up in. I found her passport though, tucked away among her handkerchiefs, and I've brought it along."

Collier took it from him and turned over the leaves. "Two short visits to France, eh, and then nearly a year in the United States. She came back in August. I wonder what she was doing there."

"I got a line on that from the landlady. Miss Greville told her she had been to Hollywood but had no luck there."

Collier was studying the passport photograph. "I've seen her before. A younger, fresher edition. She was a photographic model, wasn't she? Try the advertising agencies with this picture, Duffield."

The sergeant made a note. "So far it doesn't make sense," he remarked. "I mean, where's the motive?"

"She seems to have been the sort of woman who can make a lot of trouble," said Collier slowly. "The kind men lose their heads over. Or perhaps I should say, she has been. She's over forty and has lived hard, and she was beginning to slip. If we could find any evidence of attempted blackmail—"

Duffield brightened. "I'll get on to the advertising agencies, like you said."

"Yes. And ring up Mr. Kent. You ought to be able to get him at the school. Ask him for the name of the friend at whose studio he first met her, and look him up. Try to catch the 6.15 down to Scanbridge. I hope to go back on that. There's a restaurant car and we can get some grub. I'm off now to interview Mr. Morosini."

"You might tell him both the cloakroom taps need new washers," said Duffield.

Collier grinned. "Yes. I'm going in that spirit."

CHAPTER VI
TRANSIT OF VENUS

MR. MOROSINI's studio flat was on the ground floor of one of the fine old Georgian houses overlooking Regent's Park. The door was opened by a stout and swarthy elderly woman dressed in black who eyed Collier suspiciously.

"You cannot see Mr. Morosini. He is not here."

"When will he be back?"

"I do not know."

She was about to close the door when Collier inserted his foot. "Just a moment," he said pleasantly. "I know Mr. Morosini is a busy man, but this is a police matter and it concerns his school." He showed her his warrant. "Was he here for lunch?"

He saw that she was impressed and perhaps a little frightened. Her manner changed and became less combative.

"A light lunch, yes. An omelette, gnocchi, a glass of Chianti. He was working all the morning, a lady came to sit for her portrait. But now he is gone. He said 'I may not return to-night'. He did not take a suitcase so I think maybe he go back to Bello Sguardo. We had heard there was trouble. Beppi rang up last night."

"Was Mr. Morosini upset?"

"He was angry. He broke a vase, a beautiful vase from the Fattoria Cantegalli. Poum. Like that. He cannot paint if he is worried. He has worries enough with his sitters. Often they are ugly and they want to look beautiful. And then friends see the picture and they say 'Darling, how marvellous, but—somehow—it is not you—' and then there are—how you say—hair on the common."

Collier grinned. "Hair? Oh, I get it. Wigs on the green. Well, thanks very much."

"Niente," she said graciously.

"I'm a great admirer of his work," said Collier. "I wonder if I might be allowed just a peep inside his studio?"

He had overcome her initial hostility. It was clear that she was alone in the flat and dying for someone to talk to. Her hesitation was only momentary. She stepped back and allowed him to pass into the large and lofty studio which, in Victorian days, had been the billiard room. There were good rugs on the polished floor and some well-cushioned divans, but the colours were subdued and the general effect was less ornate than Collier had anticipated. A large canvas had been left on an easel. It represented a young girl in a backless evening dress of black chiffon over cloth of silver. She seemed to be turning away and glancing back over her shoulder at the spectator while her hand was raised to lift the folds of a curtain of deep rose-coloured brocade.

"Bellissima, n'e vero?" said Romilda proudly.

Collier drew a long breath. The woman was right. It was a lovely thing. Much might be forgiven to the man who could paint such a picture. He said, "You're right. Who is she? I seem to know that face."

"It is Mr. Morosini's fidanzata. Lady Violet Easedal."

The devil it is, thought Collier. No wonder her face seemed familiar. One of the most beautiful debutantes of the Coronation year, the sister-in-law of a Cabinet Minister, she was a much-photographed young woman. She had been engaged to a duke, but the engagement was broken off three weeks after it was announced. Collier remembered that Kent had said that Morosini was reported to be going to marry one of his aristocratic sitters. Interesting but probably irrelevant. He thanked the housekeeper again and withdrew.

He got on a bus at Baker Street. He had some time on his hands and might as well use it in trying to pick up some trace of Althea Greville's more recent activities. Duffield's reference to Hollywood had given him an idea. He called at the office of a theatrical and film agency in Shaftesbury Avenue and was shown at once into the manager's office.

"All right, Levy," he said, as they shook hands. "Nothing for you to worry about. I just want to know if you have a woman named Althea Greville on your books. She may have been trying to crash the movie studios."

"Lately?"

"She came back from the States in August."

"I do not recall the name, but there are so many—"

He had a book brought to him and ran his finger down the page.

"Yes. Early in September. I remember now. I saw her myself. She had something, but she was no longer young. I could not hold out much hope, but I put her name down for crowd work. She used to call, but she hasn't been in lately. I was sorry for her."

"Would you say she was attractive?"

"She had been. She moved well. So few women do. Put up a good bluff too, though she couldn't fool me. I've had too much experience. She was near the end of her tether. And now I suppose she's done something, or you wouldn't be enquiring after her."

But Collier thanked him and took his leave without satisfying his curiosity. Time was passing and he wanted to see his superintendent at the Yard before meeting Duffield at Victoria.

Cardew sat hunched up at his desk, in a blue haze of tobacco smoke, initialling forms. He glanced up as the younger man came in. "Cleaned up?"

"Far from it."

"Well, sit down and tell me all about it."

Collier outlined the case.

Cardew grunted. "Might have been wished on you by your worst enemy. Do you suspect anybody, apart from evidence, which, apparently, doesn't exist?"

"Not really. Kent may know her better than he cares to admit, and he's obviously worried. I haven't seen the other master or Morosini yet. I've a notion that though she hasn't tried blackmail yet she might have been making a start. Hollis is more or less dependent on his wife, and Morosini is engaged to a Society lovely. Then there's the caretaker, another unknown quantity. I don't say he's staying in bed to avoid me, but he may be. He's an ex-service man, badly wounded and gassed in the last war, poor devil, and he is subject to what his wife calls bad turns, during which she does his work. She found that he had crocked up rather suddenly when she came home from her shopping on Wednesday evening. She had to get him hot bottles and so forth so she left the locking up of the school building until some time later, and did not go through the place, just ran up the drive in the dark and turned the key in the main door. I fancy the locking up is always perfunctory. There's nothing in the dump worth stealing."

"Haven't you anything positive?"

Collier hesitated. "I think I'm safe in assuming some connection with the school," he said at last. "That narrows things down a bit."

"Have the locals any ideas on the subject?"

"The C.C. does not want Mr. Morosini to be rubbed up the wrong way. He subscribes liberally to all the local funds. I think he feels that if any tactless enquiries have to be made, leading to a stink, they had better be carried out by the Yard, and that's why they were so prompt in calling us in."

Cardew grunted. "Four main suspects. If I were you I should get a detailed statement from each one of them of what he did on Wednesday from four o'clock until he went to bed. She may have been killed some time later than you think. It's possible, you know, that she was meeting some-body at the school after hours."

"I'll bear that in mind, sir. I had been thinking of work-ing on those lines, but I can't do anything about Hollis. He's got concussion, besides minor injuries. They brought him home in an ambulance this morning, and he's got two nurses."

"Well, he can't run away. You're down about this case, aren't you, my boy?"

Collier admitted that he was, but he was in better spir-its when he left to catch his train. Cardew, stout, flabby, slow in speech, did not either look or sound brilliant, but there was something about his placidity under the most adverse circumstances that gave the younger men who worked under him confidence. They knew that he would never let them down.

Sergeant Duffield had something of the same quality and Collier, who was occasionally apt to let a vivid imagination run away with him, sometimes referred to him as his brake. The two men met by the barrier five minutes before their train was due to leave. Collier found an empty compartment while the sergeant fetched cups of tea and ham sandwiches from a trolley. Ten minutes later, as the train gathered way, they both lit their pipes and Duffield made his report.

"I rang up Mr. Kent at the school, and he made no bones about giving me the name and address of the friend where he first met the deceased. It's in Chelsea, a block of studios off the King's Road. Aloysius Bran is the name. He answered the door to me himself. A big, beefy, hearty chap with a voice like a foghorn. Quite civil he was and anxious to help. He said Althea Greville called on him last year to ask for work. He doesn't use models much, but he recommended her to friends and she came to a few of his studio binges. He didn't know Kent had engaged her for the Morosini School until he read about the murder in yesterday's *Daily Mail*. He said she was very well known ten or fifteen years ago. She was the favourite model of somebody called Ambrose Lampeter, who was a big noise in the art world, and she was a tremendous draw at a very exclusive night club—the Shut Eye—doing a turn called plastic poses. But Lampeter drank himself to death, and afterwards she began to go to pieces. Bran said, 'Damnably attractive, but a damned fool, and made enemies of the other women because of her poaching habits.' There was a row at his place when she tried to annex somebody's boy friend, and she didn't come again. Bran said he wouldn't have been surprised to see her in the gutter selling matches. She was bound to go down."

"Did you ask him if she ever worked for Morosini in her palmy days?"

"I did. He said he wouldn't know. She used to go about with Lampeter, but she probably sat for other people. I've been thinking has it occurred to you that the crime might have been committed by a woman?"

"It has."

Neither of them spoke for a moment. Both were remembering the faded anxious little face and the sinewy work-worn hands of Mrs. Pearce lying clasped on her lap as she sat facing them in her chilly unused parlour, while her husband tossed and turned on his bed in the room above.

Collier cleared his throat. "I'll tell you what I've got—"

He outlined his recent activities. "We'll make the Green Man our headquarters for the present," he said. "I'll see if I can catch Morosini at home this evening. Meanwhile I've got an ordnance map of the district. I want you to study it and make a plan of the route you would have taken if you had done the job and wanted to get home as quickly as possible and unobserved. Home being any one of three spots about equidistant from the centre of your unlawful goings on. We'll go over the ground to-morrow."

"Very good, sir."

It was a few minutes past eight when Collier flashed his torch over the fine wrought-iron work of the gates of Bello Sguardo and made his way up the drive to the villa.

The Italian manservant opened the door and admitted him at once to the hall where the Venetian lanterns hanging from the vaulted ceiling glimmered overhead and the silence was only broken by the trickle of water in the fountain.

"Can I see Mr. Morosini?"

"I am so sorry, Inspector. The padrone is expected, but he has not yet arrived. Are you staying in the village?"

"Yes."

"I could ring you up when he comes, and if it is late perhaps you would be good enough to defer your visit until to-morrow morning? Or he may speak to you himself. I am only a servant. I do not know what he will wish to do."

"All right," said Collier rather curtly. Beppi's manners had improved but the man from the Yard, who had a considerable experience of liars, did not feel at all sure that Morosini himself was not somewhere within hearing. "But will you tell your master that if he can't make it convenient to see me by nine o'clock to-morrow morning at the latest, I'm afraid he may be required to come along to police headquarters at Scanbridge to answer a few questions. Good evening."

He decided to call at The Laurels and try to see Mrs. Hollis. There was nothing foreign or fantastic about the Hollis ménage. The door was opened by an elderly parlourmaid and Collier was shown into a breakfast-room in which a good deal had evidently been spent on comfort. Collier eyed the easy chairs wistfully. He knew his wife had been planning to give him one for a birthday present but the price was prohibitive and he had made a valiant effort to persuade her that another and more inexpensive make would do just as well. On the other hand, the pictures hanging on the walls were not the kind of thing an artist would be likely to put up with if he had any voice in the matter. Collier recalled what he had learned of Hollis. The landlord of the Green Man had said with a chuckle, "He married money. Miss Folliott up at The Laurels. Some folks has all the luck. But they say she makes him toe the line. He used to drop in here for a pint, but not since he married, oh, no!"

"You wished to see me?"

Mrs. Hollis was a tall, slim woman, very upright, with regular features, beautifully waved grey hair, and frosty blue eyes. A woman, thought Collier, with a great deal of self-control. He said, "I am sorry to trouble you at such a moment. I understand that Mr. Hollis met with an accident."

"In Leicester Square. Yes. He is apt to take unnecessary risks in the traffic. He will be laid up for some weeks. Fortunately it was no worse."

"I am in charge of the enquiry into the death of the model at the school, and I had been hoping Mr. Hollis could help me."

"Indeed. In what way?"

Her tone was glacial and Collier, who was not easily disconcerted, moved uneasily.

"Might we sit down?"

"I prefer to stand. My time is very limited. I may be wanted upstairs. I do not care to leave my husband for long."

"I will not keep you long. Mr. Hollis was at the school on Wednesday afternoon?"

"I believe so. He left the house as usual, soon after lunch. I took my dog for a walk. I went as far as Engle Green where I called on a friend, a Miss Brough. She breeds dogs, Cairns and Irish setters, and I bought Patrick from her. She persuaded me to stay to tea, and I did not get home until after dark. I do not mind that. I am country bred. I was born and brought up here and know my way about."

"Mr. Hollis had his tea alone then?"

"I suppose so. My shoes were very muddy and I went straight up to my room, to rest before dinner. I had a bath and changed. I heard him come up later on and move about in his dressing-room, but I did not see him until I went down to the dining-room at eight."

"I see," said Collier, wondering why she troubled to answer him so fully. "Did he ever mention Miss Greville to you?"

"Is that the model? No. Never. The other master engaged the models. That is to say, the models for the life class. My husband finds people in the village to sit for the less advanced students, old-age pensioners usually, who are glad to earn a few shillings. I know he got old Stryver. The poor old man has been very inclined to mope since his son died. And now. Inspector, if you will excuse me—"

Collier had seldom been so firmly dismissed.

The parlour-maid was waiting in the hall to show him out and he spoke to her.

"Mr. Hollis had his tea alone on Wednesday, I hear. What time would that be?"

"I couldn't say, I'm sure."

"Don't you remember? He was later than usual, wasn't he?"

"He rang for tea when he came in. I don't know what time. I didn't notice."

"Would the cook remember, do you think?"

"She was out. She has Wednesday afternoons."

"I see. Thank you."

Collier reflected as he trudged down the drive that neither Mr. nor Mrs. Hollis had alibis. It was difficult to associate the idea of murder with the woman he had just left. She had obviously led the sheltered life of her class and generation. High-minded, he thought. High and narrow. As pure as ice, as hard as nails, and—where the husband she had married rather late in life was concerned—very possessive. These middle-aged infatuations sometimes took a sinister turn. He decided that he would leave her name on his list. The night was very dark but it was not raining. He thought he would call on Kent before calling it a day.

Poona, a hundred yards from the main road, was, he noticed, very imperfectly blacked out. There were lights in both ground floor rooms. Collier rang the bell and waited, and after a rather long interval a young man came out, closing the door after him.

"If this is A.R.P. again," he said, "the mater is sick of all this fuss and nonsense and so am I, and you can go and boil your heads. We've got some friends in playing bridge, and I've got to go back so you can cut the cackle."

"I have nothing to do with A.R.P.," said Collier, "though I can see you'll get into trouble if you don't screen your windows more effectively. You are young Mansfield, I suppose. Mr. Kent's nephew. Can I see Mr. Kent?"

"He's out. Gone to the Pictures at Scanbridge. He usually makes himself scarce Friday evenings when we have friends in for bridge. Gosh! Are you the cop?"

"I am. And I think I'll come in for a few minutes if you don't mind," said Collier blandly, and before the young man could make any effective protest he had opened the door and preceded him into the hall where they stood wedged between a large old-fashioned hat and umbrella stand and the foot of the stairs.

In the dim light of the hall lamp Arnold Mansfield was revealed as a boy of about nineteen whose outstanding good looks were marred by a rather unwholesome pallor and a sulky expression. Collier saw no resemblance to his uncle, and took an immediate dislike to him.

"I don't want to butt in or spoil your party," he said, "but I would like a word with Mrs. Mansfield."

"Oh—" The boy looked at him uneasily without actually meeting his eye. "She—she can't tell you anything."

"I must be the judge of that. Perhaps you would ask her to come in here."

He stepped into the shabby dining-room where he had sat and talked with Kent. A tray of coffee cups and a plate of biscuits had been set out on the table. The room had the same faint smell of the East that he had noticed before. The mantelpiece was crowded with ebony elephants and brass jugs from Benares, the second-rate junk brought home by second-rate exiles. Mrs. Mansfield came in before her son could go to fetch her.

"What is all this?" she said sharply. "Really, Arnold, I don't know what our guests will think of you. You weren't here when they arrived, and we've hardly begun to play when you leave us—"

"I'm sorry, mater—"

"I'm afraid it is my fault," said Collier agreeably. "I am Detective-Inspector Collier and I'm in charge of the enquiry into the circumstances of the death of a young woman on Wednesday evening at the Morosini school."

"We know nothing about it. I suppose you wanted to see my half-brother, Mr. Kent. He's out, unfortunately. You'll find him at the school in the morning," said Mrs. Mansfield in the tone she used when addressing agents for vacuum cleaners. "We are playing bridge and are in the middle of a game."

Collier smiled gently but held his ground. He knew her. He had watched her type in the bargain basements of London stores on the first day of a Sale, going into action like a human tank.

"I won't keep you long, Mrs. Mansfield. Just a few routine questions. Where were you on Wednesday afternoon?"

"I don't admit that you have any right to force your way in like this, Inspector, but I don't mind answering. I was at the vicarage from about three until nearly ten o'clock. The vicar is getting up a play for Christmas and I am helping with the production. Some of us meet there on Wednesdays to make the dresses and the crowns and so forth."

"Thank you. Was your son with you?"

"Arnold? No."

Collier looked at the young man who answered sulkily. "I went over to Scanbridge and spent a couple of hours at the flicks. Came home about nine. The fire was out so I went to bed."

"Did you go in by bus?"

"No. On my bike."

"Did you meet any friends in Scanbridge?"

"No."

"Was your uncle here when you came in?"

"He was not."

"Which picture house did you go to?"

"The Imperial in the High Street."

Collier thanked them both and took his leave. Mrs. Mansfield had a cast-iron alibi, but he had never supposed that the murder had been committed by a woman, though it was not, of course, impossible. Arnold Mansfield, on the other hand, might have some difficulty in producing witnesses for his. His manner was unfortunate and was bound to create prejudice. But he was not a student at the Morosini school and there was nothing to show that he had ever met Althea Greville.

He found Duffield waiting for him in the private sitting-room which the landlord of the Green Man had put at their disposal, and he was glad to find a roaring fire and to hear that the sergeant had ordered a hot supper of sausages and mashed. During the meal and afterwards, as they smoked their pipes, with their feet on the fender, they discussed the case.

"It was either Kent or Morosini," said the sergeant, "but we aren't going to be able to prove it."

"I wonder!" Collier yawned. "I think I'll turn in."

There was a knock at the door and the landlord put in his head. "You're wanted on the telephone, sir, if you don't mind coming down. It's the Scanbridge police station, and they say it's urgent."

Collier looked at his watch. It was a quarter to eleven. He groaned. "All right. I'm coming."

CHAPTER VII
DEATH AT THE PICTURES

THE Corona was a small picture-house, catering for the people who would rather see a good old film than a poor one fresh from the Hollywood mint, and that week it was showing one of the earlier successes of that agile pair, Fred Astaire and Ginger Rogers. At half-past ten the lights went up and the audience exchanged the overheated fug heavy with cigarette smoke in which they had spent the last three hours for the clammy chill of a November night. The last stragglers had gone out and the manager was in the vestibule talking to the commissionaire, when both men were startled by a loud scream which seemed to come from above. The manager was half-way up the stairs when a white-faced usherette appeared and flung herself into his arms.

"Oh, Mr. Moss—up there—in the balcony. I thought she—I put my hand on her—"

"There, there—pull yourself together—" He patted her on the back and looked round anxiously at the grinning commissionaire. "Don't stand gaping there, man. Call some of the other girls to look after her. Damn it, what's the use of having them trained for A.R.P. if they can't cope with plain hysterics."

Two other young women in the smart red and green uniform of the Corona's staff who had been on duty on the ground floor, arrived.

"Please, Mr. Moss, we heard somebody call out—"

"I know, I know," he said irritably. "It was Miss What-is-it here. Something scared her. Take her into the ladies' room and give her a dose of sal volatile or something while Byrne and I go up to the balcony and find out what is wrong—if anything—"

As the three girls moved away, the latest arrivals supporting their sobbing colleague, Byrne looked after them curiously. His grin had faded. "Beg pardon, sir. I happened to notice there was a red smear on her hand. It looked like—"

"Nonsense," snapped the manager. "Red varnished nails. Come on. We don't want to be here all night."

The Corona was not a large theatre and there were only twelve rows of seats in the balcony. The slope was rather steep and there was a gangway down the centre. The lighting, even when all the lights were on, was not very bright, but it sufficed to show that one member of the audience, a woman, had stayed behind. She occupied a seat at the far end of the last row but one on the right and was sitting huddled up as if she were asleep. The balcony seats were the most expensive and Mr. Moss did not want to offend a patron. "Excuse me, madam—" he began in his most dulcet tones as he edged his way along the row.

The commissionaire, waiting in the gangway, saw him stop abruptly and back away from her.

"Good God! Byrne! Ring up the police. Ask them to come at once. Say it's as bad as it can be. Tell the girls they can't go home. Quick—"

"Very good, sir."

Byrne hurried down to the box-office and the telephone, stopping on his way at the door of the dressing-room where the usherettes were scrambling out of their uniforms to shout, "Nobody to leave the premises. Manager's orders."

Mr. Moss, meanwhile, went rather unsteadily into his private office and had a drink. He had never needed one more.

The shrill chatter in the dressing-room had been silenced by the voice of Byrne. The girl who had given the alarm was still sniffing and choking, unable to give any coherent account of what had happened in the balcony, where her job had been to look round for gloves, scarves or any other odds and ends left behind before she switched off the lights. She was always excitable and rather fool-ish and they had not taken her seriously, but now they crowded round her. "What's up, Doris? What did you see? Tell us—"

Someone whispered, "What's that on her hand?"

"For God's sake. Wash it off, kid. Quick, run some hot water—"

"No. Don't say, anything. Leave her alone—"

The circle round her widened as they drew away.

Meanwhile the police were arriving. First two constables from the station, which was only a hundred yards away, and then Inspector Pearson, who had gone home for supper and was just letting out the cat when the telephone bell rang. Doctor Anderson came five minutes later, and after a word with the white-faced manager who was hanging about the vestibule, wilting under the cold official eye of the policeman on duty at the door, ran up the stairs to the balcony two at a time.

He was coming down again more slowly when Collier and Duffield entered the vestibule.

"So they sent for you, did they?" He beckoned to them to follow him into the auditorium, out of hearing of the manager and commissionaire. "Murder," he said. "A young woman, and she's been stabbed in the neck just as the other was. Been dead some time. I should say two or three hours at least. It could be done, you know, easily, from the seat behind. Hardly any risk. People are watching the film, or, in the back seats, making love."

Pearson joined them. His complexion looked blotchy and he was wiping his brow. He greeted Collier eagerly and without any trace of his former hostility.

"You've heard? Seems as if we had to look for a homicidal maniac. A frightful business. The question is—it's very late—can we let the staff go, or should we get statements from them now?"

"We need not keep them all," Collier said. "I suggest the girl in the box office, the usherette on duty in the balcony, the manager and the commissionaire. The rest can leave."

Pearson nodded. "That's what I thought." He hurried away.

Anderson glanced at the two men from the Yard. "Poor old Pearson. He'll be glad of your help. We don't go in much for capital crime in these parts. And he's right, you know. If this is the work of a killer with a complex about young women, it's nasty. He may strike at any time, anywhere."

"I'll just go up and have a look at her," said Collier. "You, too, Duffield. You'll be here when we come down, Doctor? We shan't be long."

"I suppose so," said the doctor grumpily.

"Has she been identified?"

"Nobody I know, thank the Lord."

The lights were on upstairs. Collier looked about him thoughtfully before moving along the back row of tip-up velvet-covered seats to get a close up view of the balcony's solitary occupant. He saw at once that this girl was of a different type to the first victim. Her dark brown tweed coat and brown cloth beret were of good material and warm but not showy. There was no paint on the still face, a small sallow face with irregular features. A pair of horn-rimmed spectacles had slipped off and lay on her lap. The front of the dark coat was sodden with blood. Her brown hand-knitted woollen gloves lay on the floor.

Collier said nothing. The sergeant, glancing at him, saw a look on his face that boded ill for someone. They went downstairs again. The constable on duty at the entrance told them that Inspector Pearson was in the manager's office.

The doctor had gone.

"He said he hoped you wouldn't mind. There's nothing more he can do to-night, and he's expecting an urgent call. The ambulance will be here any minute, but I'm having some photographs taken first and measurements."

"Yes. Yes, of course."

"I've sent the girls home, all but the one who found the body. I had to let one of my chaps go with them. They were afraid of being set upon, and you can't blame them."

Collier nodded. "Let's have the manager in first."

Mr. Moss was anxiously polite. He would give every possible assistance.

"May we reopen as usual to-morrow?"

"Yes. But you must not use the balcony for a day or two."

The manager's face fell. "That will mean a loss of a third of our takings."

"Is the balcony much used?"

"Hardly at all in some houses, but ours is very popular with our patrons."

"How do you account for the fact that nobody noticed anything wrong until the place was cleared?"

"Our programme is continuous. The lights go on at the end of a picture, but only for a minute. She was at the end of the row and no one would have to pass her."

"I see. Do you find one usherette enough up there?"

"Normally we have two, but we are short-handed, two girls away with 'flu."

"The girl who was on duty to-night—what's her name?"

"Fleet. Doris Fleet."

"Has she been with you long?"

"About eighteen months."

"You have been satisfied with her?"

"Oh, quite. She is civil and obliging and, I am sure, quite honest. Her parents keep a little sweet shop in Church Row. Most respectable people, I believe."

"Yes, yes," said Pearson impatiently, "I know the Fleets. They're all right. Now, I suppose you are in and out of your office during the evening. You don't happen to have noticed anyone leaving in a hurry? The balcony people would have to pass through this vestibule, wouldn't they?"

"Yes. No, I can't say I did. Byrne might have. But he has to keep an eye on the queue waiting to come in after the first house, and our lights are heavily shaded. The black-out, you know. You could ask Miss Lamb, the young lady in the box office."

"Thanks, I will. You might send her in here now. I won't keep you much longer, Mr. Moss."

But Miss Lamb had noticed nothing unusual, and neither had the commissionaire. Doris Fleet came last on the list. She had recovered to some extent, though she was still very white under the hastily applied makeup. She sat on the edge of the chair that had been placed for her and answered the questions Pearson asked her shakily.

She didn't remember showing a young woman in a brown coat and beret to a seat at the end of the last row but one. Some of the older people were very helpless in the dark and had to be led, but the younger ones looked after themselves. It was all one price in the balcony so it did not matter where they went. She had to tear off half each ticket.

"Was every seat occupied this evening?"

"Oh, no. The front rows were full."

"What about the back row of all? Try to remember?"

She frowned with the effort of concentration. "I don't know. There's seldom more than a sprinkling like. People say it's draughty. Mostly—" she broke off awkwardly.

"Mostly—yes—go on, Miss Fleet."

"I—I was going to say they're mostly courting couples who don't bother about the pictures. We—we call that row lovers' lane. Oh—please don't ask me any more! I want to forget it. I could never bear to be up there in the dark again. Mum. Dad. I want to go home—"

"There, there, don't upset yourself." The burly inspector could be quite fatherly when the need arose. "You can run along now. Miss Lamb lodges next door to you, doesn't she, so you can go together."

"Nothing to help us so far," said Pearson, pessimistically when he came back, after shepherding the weeping Doris into the vestibule.

"I've let the manager and Byrne go. I told them we should probably be able to let their cleaners in to-morrow at eleven."

Collier nodded. "You'll have to go through all the lockers and so forth. There's a chance, you know, that the murder was committed by one of the staff."

Pearson stared at him. "But how could one of the people employed here have killed Althea Greville? It doesn't make sense."

"No. But it may when we know a little more. Is this the poor girl's handbag? We may see light somewhere when we know who she is."

"You'll take this on, I hope," said Pearson eagerly. "I'm sure the C.C. will wish it, and you can rely on us all to help you up to the limit. Anderson told you what he thinks? I hope to God he's wrong. Almost anything would be better than a homicidal maniac at large. In that case there needn't be any motive that a sane man would recognise. And what can we do with the black-out—"

"Nothing much, I'm afraid," said Collier, "but I don't agree with Doctor Anderson. I fancy the killer is sane. No murderer is entirely so, you know. Shall we say sane enough to qualify for the eight o'clock walk, and not for Broadmoor. And now about this bag—"

CHAPTER VIII
THE WAY YOU LOOK TO-NIGHT!

AT SEVEN o'clock Miss Haydon's prim elderly maid came into her bedroom with a cup of tea and a can of hot water.

"Please, miss—"

Miss Haydon switched on the light by her bedside. "Dear me, Emma, you're very early. This isn't the morning I go to the eight o'clock celebration—"

"No, miss, but there's a man downstairs."

"A man? What do you mean? If it's gas or electricity tell him to go away and come again at a reasonable hour."

"Please, miss, it's the police."

"Good heavens. A policeman—"

"Not exactly," said Emma, with a sniff. "He's not in uniform, but he showed me a card. He's an Inspector from Scotland Yard."

"Oh dear," said Miss Haydon. "I hope—very well, Emma. I'll get dressed at once. Ask him to wait." Her hands shook as she fumbled over her clothes. What could it be? A friend of hers had been ruined years ago by a defaulting solicitor. She thought of her lawyers. They seemed such nice men, but one never knew. Or—she had some small house property. Suppose one of her tenants—"This," thought Miss Haydon, as she slipped in her false teeth, "is where one feels a man in the house might be of some use."

The Inspector was in the drawing-room where Emma, very rightly, had lit the gas fire. He was standing by the window and looking across the smooth green turf of the Close at the long silvery roof and the soaring towers of the cathedral. He turned as Miss Haydon came in, and she saw that he was a man in his middle thirties, with a slight but active figure and a lean face, tanned by wind and weather. As she would have expressed it, he looked like a gentleman.

"You wished to see me? I hope it isn't anything very bad—"

He looked down at the plump, wrinkled, rather foolish face, one of the vast majority of neutral faces belonging to people whose little niggling faults are offset by little niggling virtues, and said gently, "I am afraid I must give you a shock. Won't you sit down?"

"I—very well. Won't you?"

"Thank you."

"It is so very early. I suppose that means it is urgent—"

"You have a niece living with you, Miss Haydon. Didn't you expect her home last night?"

"Betty? I thought she was staying with her friend. She does sometimes. What has happened? Not—not run over—"

"What friend would that be, Miss Haydon?"

"Cherry Garth. Quite a nice girl, or I shouldn't allow it. She has been over here to tea with Betty. They are fellow students at Morosini's—"

"I see. Did she leave here to go to the school as usual yesterday?"

"So far as I know. I am a very busy woman, Mr.—er—"

"Collier."

"There is the canteen work and the W.V.S. They rely on me to do the cutting out. I'm hardly ever home for lunch. Perhaps I had better ring for Emma. But I wish you would tell me what has happened to the child—"

Collier rang the bell, and the elderly maid appeared so promptly that he suspected that she had been listening at the door.

"Did Miss Betty go off at the usual time, Emma?"

"No, ma'am. She called to me as soon as you was out of the house that she'd have her breakfast in bed. I asked her, when I took up the tray, if she was feeling poorly. She said she was all right, but in no hurry to go back to the school."

"Did she say why?" asked Collier.

"She said there had been what she called a bust up, and she didn't want to be mixed up in it. I said 'Of course not, miss, but why should you be?' And she said 'Because of what I saw.' I said 'What was that?' But she only laughed and said that would be telling."

"She laughed?" said Collier. He felt then that whatever Betty Haydon thought she knew it could not have been the truth.

"She meant no harm," said Emma quickly. "Oh dear, I hope she hasn't got into no trouble through holding back. I warned her. I said if it was a police matter she ought to help not to hinder them, especially as it had been going on some time and ought to be cleared up."

"You knew about it then?" said Collier.

At this point Miss Haydon intervened as Collier had feared she might. "Miss Betty seems to have told you a great deal more than she did me," she said in an offended voice.

Luckily Emma stood in no awe of her employer and answered jauntily that maybe she did. "And no wonder. You're too wrapped up in your alphabet to have any time for your own flesh and blood."

"Alphabet?" murmured Collier.

"Wops or Wrens, or whatever it is, and I daresay they do very good work," said Emma handsomely.

Collier brought her back to the point. "What was the trouble at the school?"

"Why the pilfering that's been going on since the beginning of the term, money taken from pockets of coats left in the cloakrooms and odds and ends from the lockers." She looked up at him suddenly. "If you are the police you must know. I made sure a trap had been set and somebody caught—"

"Just a moment," said Collier. "Let's get back to yesterday. I have a reason for wanting to know as much as possible of Miss Betty's doings. Didn't she go to the school at all?"

"She went by a train that would get her there about noon. She said she didn't feel like working anyway, but she wanted to see her friend, Miss Garth, and maybe they'd have lunch together and she'd try and persuade her to go on what she called a razzle afterwards."

"What did she mean by a razzle?"

"Well, I daresay they'd go in to Scanbridge and look at the shops and have tea at the Cadena and finish up at the pictures. I know that's what they did the day before. They saw something then that Miss Betty was hankering to see again. She's got what they call a pash for that Fred Astaire. I heard her humming one of the tunes. She's got a record of it. 'The way you look to-night'." Emma paused and swallowed hard. "What—what's happened to Miss Betty, sir?"

"I'm sorry," he said slowly.

Miss Haydon clutched at her maid's hand and quavered "Oh, Emma!"

They would have to know the truth sooner or later. He told them that Betty Hayden's body had been found in the balcony of the Corona picture house at the close of the performance.

"Last night, about ten hours ago. We established her identity through the railway season ticket between Elder Green and Scanminster which was found in her handbag, but by that time it was so late that we thought it best to wait for the morning to break the bad news."

Miss Haydon blew her nose. She looked white and shaken but she had achieved a certain dignity. "Are you trying to tell me that my poor niece was murdered?"

"I am afraid there is no doubt about that, Miss Haydon."

"But why—unless she was attacked by a madman—"

"We don't know yet, but we shall. Thank you, Miss Haydon. There will have to be an inquest. We'll let you know about that. Meanwhile, could you give me the address of her friend, Miss Garth?"

"Number Seven, Victoria Terrace, Elder Green. She is in lodgings. It is not far from the station, on the road to the village."

Emma saw him out. He paused at the door and said, "Was Miss Betty happy here? Did she get on with her aunt?"

"Well enough. Miss Haydon is out all day, but so was Miss Betty; they didn't see enough of each other to quarrel."

"Any love affair?"

Emma answered decidedly. "None. Miss Betty was wrapped up in her film stars. She was shy of real boys. And she wasn't one to attract them. A born old maid if you ask me. Why? It—it couldn't have been suicide, could it?"

"No. How old was she?"

"Nineteen."

Collier's face was grim as he made his way back to the station. The poor child, he thought, the poor harmless, chattering little fool, boasting of the knowledge that was her death warrant.

He caught a train crowded with business men on their way up to Town, and was the only passenger to alight at Elder Green ten minutes later. It was, as he had ascertained, the train by which Betty Haydon usually went, and as he walked up the road he saw a girl come out of the last house in the row of ugly little red brick villas on his left, and wait by the gate. She was looking past him towards the station, evidently expecting her friend. She was not pretty, but she had a round, good-tempered face and Collier, who hated lipstick, noticed that her mouth was a natural healthy red. He stopped to speak to her, disliking his task.

"Excuse me, but are you Miss Garth?"

"Yes. What is it—"

He said, "I am sorry. I'm afraid I have some bad news for you. You lodge here, I think. Have you a sitting-room?"

"Yes. But—I shall be late for school—"

"I shall not keep you long. You know who I am. You were there yesterday when I spoke to the assembled students."

"Yes, of course. I didn't recognise you at first. I wasn't expecting to see you. Please come in. We shall not be disturbed. My landlady goes out to work, and there isn't anyone in the house."

He followed her into the little front sitting-room, furnished with a cheap three-piece suite and an aspidistra on a bamboo stand. The only signs of Cherry's occupation were a few books on a shelf, a work-bag with a half-finished jumper exuding from it, and a couple of unframed sketches pinned to the walls.

"Please sit down," she said, "and smoke if you want to. There are cigarettes in that box on the mantelpiece." He suppressed a smile. She reminded him of a child playing at receiving visitors. His smile faded as he recalled the nature of his business. He was about to give her a frightful shock. Even now he thought she looked anxious. Naturally enough. He was the police.

He said, "You were waiting for Miss Haydon just now?"

"Yes. We generally walk up to the school together. But I suppose she missed the train."

"Did you see her yesterday?"

"Yes. But she came over very late, after you had gone. The morning session was just over. We went over to Mrs. Meggott's for a spot of lunch, and I told her what had been happening. She didn't say much, but I could see she was upset. I wanted her to come back to the school and speak to Mr. Kent and get him to ring up the police station at Scanbridge, but she said she must think it over. She said she didn't feel like working and she wanted to see *Swing Time* again and she asked me to go in to Scanbridge with her. It's an old film revived and it's on this week at the Corona, but we had been there together the day before, and once was enough for me."

"Do you often go to the pictures with her?"

"Sometimes. She goes more often than I do. I'm living in digs so I can't afford to spend so much."

"What part of the house do you usually go to?"

"The balcony at the Corona, and Betty likes to sit far back because she's long sighted."

"I suppose you see the same people there time and again, regular patrons, what?"

"I'm afraid I haven't noticed. Why are you asking all these questions. Has—has anything happened to Betty?"

He answered gravely, "Yes. It would have been better, Miss Garth, if she had taken your advice and got into touch with us. She knew something, didn't she, bearing on the murder of Althea Greville?"

She sat gazing at him, and he saw that she had turned very white.

"Are you trying to tell me—Betty isn't—"

"She was found last night in the back row but one of the balcony at the Corona. She had been killed at some time during the performance."

"How—how horrible. Oh, poor Betty—" her voice broke.

"Yes," he said, "it is horrible. A vile and cowardly crime. And that is why you are going to do your best to help us bring the murderer to book. She knew something. Did she tell you what that something was?"

"No. She wouldn't. You see, that first day we had no idea there had been a murder. We didn't know, but we thought they might have found out who had been stealing things from the cloakrooms and the lockers, and that it would be unpleasant, and we didn't want to have to give evidence or anything. At least, I think that was what Betty thought. She liked to be mysterious and say 'Ha! Ha!' and 'I could a tale unfold!' and that sort of rot. What happened was that on Wednesday afternoon she forgot her scarf and ran back to get it while I walked slowly on down the road. When she caught up with me she was out of breath. She didn't say anything at the time, but the next morning when we weren't allowed to go into the school she hinted that she had seen someone lurking about who shouldn't have been there. At least that was the impression I got."

Collier was disappointed. "That's all you can tell me?"

"I'm afraid so."

He thought a moment. "Did she talk in the same way to other people?"

"Not in my hearing. You see, we're both rather new, and the older students don't take much notice of us."

"At this place where you had lunch, were there other people in the room?"

"No. It's only a cottage. Mrs. Meggott only does teas really, but she rather favours us."

"You were discussing the matter during your meal?"

"Yes, we were."

"Are you quite sure that you weren't overheard? This may be important."

"I can't say that. Mrs. Meggott was in and out from the kitchen and some of her own people were there. It's a large family. There's her old father, and a niece. Heaps of them. But they wouldn't bother to listen. The old man's deaf anyway, or pretends to be. He's a crusty old thing. And there's the shop where she sells sweets and minerals and cigarettes. She's got a slot machine for gaspers so people just come in and out without bothering her."

Collier sighed. It was one of those cases where every clue crumbled like sand and slipped through his fingers as he grasped it.

She looked at him anxiously. "Does it matter so much?"

"No, no. Don't let it worry you. Only—I don't want to frighten you, Miss Garth, but for your own sake I have to be rather brutally frank. If the murderer overheard your conversation then he may have gathered that Miss Haydon had not passed on her dangerous piece of information to you. If not, he must be still uncertain on that point."

She gazed at him. "But what could Betty have known?"

"To reach the women students' cloakroom she would have to go down the long passage past the door of the life classroom, and round the corner. Suppose that on her way out she saw someone just entering or just leaving the life classroom, or perhaps lurking in one of the doorways. He might have hoped that she had not recognised him, but he dared not bank on that. Obviously, from his point of view, she must be silenced. He must have known that, for some reason, she had not come to us immediately, as she should have done. What happened after your lunch at Mrs. Meggott's cottage?"

Cherry swallowed hard. "She tried to persuade me to go in to Scanbridge with her, but I wanted to work, so I walked with her to the bus stop and left her there while I went back to school."

"Was anyone else you knew waiting for the bus?"

"I didn't notice. The stop is in the middle of the village and people come up at the last minute. I wish now I'd gone with her. Perhaps if I had—"

"You weren't to know," he said consolingly.

She blew her nose and said rather indistinctly, "I can't realise it even now."

She was not pretty, but she looked appealingly young and soft and defenceless, sitting huddled up in her cheap tweed coat with her beret pulled down over her untidy mop of fair hair.

Collier recalled the other girl as he had seen her last and bit his lip. He said abruptly "Who else is there living in this house?"

"There's only my landlady, Miss Tremlett, and me."

"I must talk to her. What sort of woman is she? Motherly? Sensible?"

"Neither, I'm afraid. But she isn't a bad old thing. We get on all right. She's out just now. She goes out to oblige."

"There's a room for another lodger?"

"Yes. But she says one is enough for her."

"I can't help that. Now listen to me, Miss Garth. I want you to stay at home to-day. More than that. I want you to go up to your bedroom and lock yourself in, and don't come out until you see me come back; I shall bring a young man with me who will have that other room and whose job it will be not to let you out of his sight. He'll be—I expect you have guessed it in one—he'll be a policeman in mufti, and his job will be to guard you. Try not to mind it. It will only be for a day or two. Your evidence at the inquest will make it clear that you know nothing that could lead to the arrest of the murderer, and after that you will be safe. But meanwhile we must take no chances."

"I see," she said. "Thank you."

He glanced round at the sketches pinned to the walls, but his thoughts were elsewhere. "You know all these people much better than I do, Miss Garth. That's always our difficulty. Have you any theory about this case? Don't be afraid of being libellous. This is unofficial. You needn't answer if you don't want to."

She reddened and answered quickly and with an anger which he realised was not for him, "I only know that what some people are saying is utterly wrong and impossible. They ought to be ashamed when he's never done them any harm, and he's always so patient—" she broke off in confusion.

Collier said quietly, "You mean Mr. Kent?"

He remembered facing the assembled students in the preliminary classroom with Kent standing by his side. He had noticed Cherry then, and the rapt lost gaze of which Kent, who was its object, had been entirely unconscious. Kent. So he was suspected by some of his own students.

He said gently, "Don't be afraid that we'll take the wrong man. That doesn't happen. And now will you go upstairs, please, and lock yourself in. And don't look out of the window until you hear me call. I'll be back within two hours."

CHAPTER IX
THE GREAT MAN

COLLIER was picked up by a police car a quarter of a mile farther up the road and taken back to Scanbridge to make his report to the Chief Constable, who had been rung up soon after seven with news of the second murder, and had come over, after a hurried breakfast, to confer with his subordinates.

"We are agreed that this is a part of your case, Inspector, but, of course, if you feel that you need more help—" he said tentatively.

"That's all right, sir. I think I can manage with Sergeant Duffield, and the assistance of your people. I want a plain clothes man now." He described his interview with Betty

Haydon's aunt and her maid, and his subsequent conversation with her friend, Cherry Garth.

Major Payne frowned, pulling at his grizzled moustache. "You think this girl is in actual danger?"

"I am afraid so. In my opinion Betty Haydon was killed because she knew something that might put us on the trail of the murderer. Whatever it was she didn't pass it on to Miss Garth, but the murderer does not know that. I should like the inquest—the second inquest—to be opened to-morrow immediately after the first. I'd like it to be well advertised in advance and fully reported in the local press afterwards."

"It will be that. Don't you fret," said the Chief Constable grimly. "They don't often have anything more exciting than a flower show or the annual Hunt ball to write about. But what's the idea? Why rush it?"

"I want Miss Garth to be called—as she would have to be eventually in any case, and I want questions asked which will make it clear that she knows nothing at all about the first affair. After that I hope she will be fairly safe, though I think she should have police protection until we have made an arrest."

"I get you," said the Major. "I think it can be managed. Both inquests will be indefinitely adjourned, of course. The coroner is a personal friend of mine. We often go round the links together. I'll ring him up."

"Thank you, sir. And meanwhile I want a man who will come along with me to Miss Garth's lodgings and stay there until further notice. I'll give him his instructions as we go."

"You'd better have Griffiths. He's a Welshman and has been nicely brought up," said the Chief Constable, apparently without any facetious intention.

"That may be useful," said Collier, with equal serious-ness. "The landlady was out and may make a fuss."

"Griffiths has a way with landladies."

The young Welshman listened respectfully to the admonitions of the Inspector from the Yard as they sat together in the back of the car on the way to Elder Green. He had only recently been promoted from the uniformed branch and he was longing to prove himself worthy. His round boyish face was red with excitement as he sat clutching the brim of his hat and saying, "Yes, sir, I under-stand," at intervals.

"You've got to stay whether the landlady wants you or not. Miss Garth will help you. She's a sensible girl. Talk it over with her and have your plan of campaign ready when the old woman comes home. And mind—Miss Garth isn't to go out without you, and no visitors are to be admitted. You'll answer the door, and if it's one of the students from the school or a member of the staff it's all the same. But get them to give you their names. There may not be anybody. We're taking precautions, that's all."

Cherry's face appeared at the upper window as the garden gate of number seven, Station Cottages, creaked on its hinges. She ran down to admit them.

"Nobody has been—"

"Good!" Collier introduced Constable Griffiths and hurried away.

It was past ten, and he was to have called at Bello Sguardo at nine. He reflected, however, that Morosini had given him a good deal of trouble, and it would do him no harm to wait.

The manservant's manner conveyed a dignified reproach, but he ushered him in silence into a vast studio where the great man was walking about, smoking ciga-rettes and evidently seething with rage.

"I have been waiting here, kicking my heels, for over an hour. Over an hour, per Bacco. I am a busy man, my time is of value. It is precious. You haven't the common civility to be punctual."

"I'm very sorry, Mr. Morosini. It couldn't be helped. I've been busy too, and my business was urgent. I've been up all night, as a matter of fact. I only took an hour off to have a bath and a shave and get a bite of breakfast—"

Morosini waved that aside as irrelevant. "Urgent," he said contemptuously. "Your values are all wrong. The pursuit of beauty is the only urgent thing in life. Nothing else matters."

He was a handsome man, with a fine profile, flashing dark eyes, and a mane of black hair which was just beginning to grow grey at the temples. In ten years' time he would be even more striking than he was now. He was not Collier's idea of a gentleman, but he was prepared to make allowances for a foreigner, even if he had been naturalised and had lived many years in England.

He sidestepped a dissertation on beauty to say stolidly, "You were here on Wednesday?"

"Wednesday? Yes, I dined here, and went up to Town afterwards. What of it?"

"Nothing, sir. Just routine questions. You weren't to know, of course, that the life model at your school had been murdered. I rather wish you had come back though directly you heard of it. Our time is worth something too—to the ratepayers."

Morosini glared. "You presume to be insolent."

"I'm sorry you take it that way, sir," said Collier patiently. "It's my duty to ask people questions. We rather expect the public to assist us, especially when we're on a murder case."

"I'm not the public."

"No, sir. You have a special interest. We recognise that."

Morosini glared at him. "What the devil do you mean by that?"

"The crime was committed in the school founded by you, in a building that is your property, a stone's throw from your own house. Did you know Althea Greville at all, Mr. Morosini?"

Morosini sat down, without asking his unwelcome visitor to do so, and lit another cigarette. "I met her years ago," he said grudgingly. "She was the fashion for a year or two, somebody's favourite model—I forget the fellow's name, he had a vogue, quite undeserved, he was a charlatan—but he's dead now, or dropped out, and she dropped out, too. Drink, probably, or dope: I certainly had no idea that she had been engaged to pose for my students."

"Would you have objected?"

"No. Why should I? I have a competent staff. I don't interfere with their arrangements."

"Can you remember what you were doing on Wednesday from four o'clock until you left for London?"

"Certainly. I was working in my library. I lunched at one, and afterwards I fenced with my man Beppi. It is good exercise and I do not want to get fat. Then I had a bath and he gave me some massage. I had a short nap and when I woke it was about half-past three. I drank a glass of orange juice and then I sat down to write. Bennstein and Lapp have asked me to let them have a book of memoirs, an autobiography. I was in the mood and I got through an important chapter dealing with my early youth. It is good, I think," he said complacently, forgetting his anger with his interlocutor in his self-satisfaction.

"I see," said Collier. "And when did you stop?"

"When Beppi came to tell me dinner was served. That was at eight. By nine I was on my way to London."

"You wrote without a break from half-past three until eight?"

"I was inspired. I am very versatile. So was Leonardo, so was Michelangelo," said Morosini with perfect seriousness.

"I suppose you told your servant you weren't to be disturbed?" suggested Collier.

"There is no need to tell him."

Collier made a mental note to find out if the library was on the ground floor. "Now about yesterday," he said. "I was sorry to miss you when I called at your flat in Regent's Park. You came down here by car, I suppose? Did you make any stop on the way? "

Either Morosini was a very good actor or he was genuinely puzzled by this enquiry.

"Of what interest can that be to the police? But I don't mind telling you." He had talked himself into a better temper. "I called for my fiancée—she is sharing a flat with a friend—we walked through the Park and had tea at the Ritz. Then she took a taxi to go home and rest before going to her canteen, and I went to the car park where I had left my car."

"When would that be?"

"Between four and five. I do not know exactly."

"I called here a few minutes after eight, Mr. Morosini, and you had not yet arrived. My information is that your car was seen to pass through the village and turn in here at twenty minutes past eleven. The drive from the West End of London here, allowing for traffic difficulties and the black-out, would hardly take more than six hours."

Morosini scowled. "I am tired of this inquisition. It is an impertinence. Intolerable. What I did and where I went yesterday cannot affect your enquiry. I shall complain to your superiors at the Yard."

"I am sorry," said Collier, but he sounded impenitent. He kept his eyes fixed on the painter's handsome spoilt face, noting his unmistakable uneasiness. Apparently they had reached a point where the truth would be inconvenient. "I have to ask these questions, Mr. Morosini, to establish what everyone who had even a remote connection with this case was doing yesterday afternoon and during the evening. There is a reason."

Morosini moistened his lips. "Indeed. What is it?"

"The body of one of your students was found in the Corona picture house at Scanbridge after the final performance."

"Good God!" If Morosini's horror was not genuine it was very well acted. "Why have I not been told of this before? This is terrible. Who is it? Why? I cannot understand what is happening here."

"Nor do we—at present. Meanwhile, Mr. Morosini, if you could give me rather a fuller account of your evening?"

Morosini rubbed out his half-smoked cigarette and took another from his case. Collier noticed that his hands were far from steady and his dark face was twitching with nervousness.

"You can't accuse me. It is ridiculous. Why must I be involved? I am an artist, a great artist. My work will suffer. As it is my school must suffer. It is abominable."

"Do you know all your students personally, Mr. Morosini?"

"No. I used to at one time, but lately I have been too much taken up with important commissions. I have an efficient staff—"

"But according to the school prospectus you watch the work of the students with a discerning eye and foster latent talent. The prospectus says that your students realise your keen personal interest in them all."

"All that was written years ago," said Morosini defensively. "And it's quite true. I look over their stuff every term and pick out the most promising."

"Do you know them all by sight?"

"I can't say that. No, I don't. What are you getting at?"

"Never mind. You left the Ritz between four and five to drive down here. How was it that you did not arrive until after eleven?"

"I had a breakdown on the road. There were no houses near. I am no use with machinery. In any case, it was dark. I thought I would wait and get a lift from another motorist, but it was cold and miserable standing by the roadside waiting. I got back into my car and wrapped my rug round me, and then I went to sleep. I was awakened by a man, a lorry driver, who got down from his lorry to find out what was wrong. He looked with a torch he had, and it was only a little thing. He put it right and I paid him well for his trouble, and I came on."

"I see," said Collier. He was quite convinced that Morosini was lying, but for the moment he accepted his statement at its face value. "Shall you be staying down here for the present? I shall want to know where I can find you if anything fresh turns up."

"Yes. I shall be here." Morosini looked relieved, as a man may who has skated over some very thin ice without hearing so much as a crack.

"I'm going over to the school now. Is there a short cut from here? I have a great deal to do in a very short time—"

"There is a way." Morosini was so glad to get rid of his visitor that he became quite genial. "I will show you."

A door in the studio opened on to a terrace. Morosini led the way across it and past a water garden where the bronze Narcissus from Herculaneum gazed pensively at the gold-fish swimming in the dark water of a pool, and through a shrubbery to a small gate opening on a field where some bullocks stopped grazing to stare at them. The raw red brick and corrugated iron of the school buildings were visible in the field beyond.

"Go straight across to the stile."

"Thank you."

"I'm afraid I was rather irritable just now. It's the shock and the worry. A terrible thing. That Greville woman, and now this poor girl—"

"What makes you think the second victim was a girl, Mr. Morosini?"

"I—I—didn't you say so?"

"I didn't. But you are quite right. She had not been at your school very long. This was her second term. She was not in the life class."

"Terrible," said Morosini again. "What possible motive in her case—it is very damp under these laurels. You must excuse me, I shall catch a cold—"

Collier did not try to detain him. Morosini had given him plenty to think about. He glanced at his watch as he closed the gate after him and again as he walked round the untidy, sprawling collection of school buildings. Say five minutes, three if you hurried, from door to door. Morosini had no real alibi for either of the relevant times.

CHAPTER X
COLLIER IS WORRIED

"HI, YOU there! What do you want?" bellowed an irate voice that reminded Collier of the barrack square.

He turned to face a man who had just emerged from the coal shed. He was a lean, angular, middle-aged man, with the sallow complexion of a bilious subject, and unhappy dark eyes. He needed a haircut and a shave, and he walked with a slight limp.

"I think you must be Pearce," said Collier.

"Sergeant Pearce to you," growled the other.

"Very well, Sergeant. I'm Detective-Inspector Collier."

Pearce blinked as if even the dull grey light of the November day was too much for him and passed his hand over his eyes. "I thought you were one of the newspaper chaps," he said. It was as near as he would ever get to an apology.

"I thought you were ill in bed."

"I was. I have bad turns. But I came down yesterday and sat by the fire, and to-day I'm back at my job."

"Have a fag?" said Collier, proffering his case.

Pearce, like so many old soldiers, was a chain smoker. The hoarse voice and the fingers deeply stained with nicotine proved it. He lit his cigarette and inhaled before he spoke again.

"So she's been done in," he said. "I can't say I'm surprised, but I wish the chap, whoever he was, had finished her off somewhere else. It's upset the wife, for one thing."

"You think she had it coming to her?"

"Sure. She was the sort that takes a man and squeezes him dry like an orange."

Collier noticed the Americanism. "Like these vamps in films," he said conversationally.

"That's right. The wife and me saw a picture not long ago. There was a girl in that on the make, grabbing, ruined the chap's life, she did. I said to the wife I'd have wrung her neck if I'd been in his place."

"How did you come to know so much about Miss Greville's character?"

"She lodged with us when she was here last year, the first time they engaged her. Never no more. She got off with more than one of the students and with chaps in the village. You'd never credit the harm a woman like that can do in three weeks."

"So you had nothing to do with her this time?"

"Nothing. She had digs in London, I believe, and come to and fro by bus. She didn't ought to have been engaged again, but Mr. Hollis and Mr. Kent didn't have no notion of what went on before, though Mr. Kent should have done, seeing as his own nephew was one of those running after her."

"Young Mansfield? But he is not a student here—"

"Not now, but he was then. Never any good though. A regular young slacker. I hear he's tried his hand at several things since then, and now he's home again for his ma to keep him—or I should say Mr. Kent."

They had come round to the front entrance where Pearce had left a pail of water and a broom.

"Any objection to me wiping over the floors in the passages?"

"None. We've been over the place for footprints and fingerprints."

"Plenty of those," said the caretaker sourly. "There's a mat and a scraper, but do those young so-and-sos ever trouble to wipe the mud off their shoes before they come in traipsing over my nice clean floors? No fear. Well, you've got to get on with your job, I suppose. I won't keep you."

Collier looked at his watch again. It was ten minutes to twelve. He had forty minutes before the end of the morning session. He walked down the corridor to Kent's room and knocked on the door. Kent's voice, pitched on a note that betrayed nervous impatience, bade him come in.

He found the junior master seated at his drawing-board. He glanced up as Collier came in. "Oh, it's you, Inspector. Please sit down. You won't mind if I go on with this. It's a commission, a design for a publisher's blurb and they're clamouring for it. I'm behind with my own work. All this upset and worry—"

Collier drew up a chair and held out his chilled hands to the blue flame of the gas fire. Kent bent over his drawing with a frown of concentration. Collier eyed him thought-fully. He knew a good deal about his circumstances, his comfortless home with greedy relations who took all he had to give and made no return, his ever present fear that the Morosini school would cease to pay its way and leave him without a job. The war would settle that, he reflected grimly, and it might do him a good turn if it freed him from his incubi. Kent was not the man to cut himself loose, he hadn't the necessary hard streak.

"I suppose I mustn't ask if you've made an arrest?"

"We haven't. How are things at the school to-day, Mr. Kent? Settling down?"

"As well as one can expect. The life class has moved into a room that has been closed since our numbers decreased three or four years ago. We couldn't get another model immediately, under the circumstances, but one of the students is sitting for the head and shoulders, so they are all right. Old Stryver hasn't turned up for the people in the Prelim, but they can always work on casts."

"Who's old Stryver?"

*"An old man from the village, a real gaffer type, with grey chin whiskers. A bit of a scrounger. He goes round selling vegetables from his allotment and he's a jobbing gardener. They say he has quite a bit of money put away,

but he's one of our regular models for our class of beginners. He's rather a dour old person, but it isn't easy to get models locally, and we're glad to have him. Have you come to give me any instructions about the inquest? I got my summons, or whatever you call it, by this morning's post."

"It won't take long. There will be an adjournment." Collier cleared his throat. "I've got some bad news for you, Mr. Kent. There's been a fresh development."

Kent finished the wash of colour he was laying on with mechanical precision and replaced his brush in the jar. "I must leave it to dry," he murmured. He seemed to brace himself. "What is it, Inspector?"

Collier told him.

Kent sat and stared at him with unconcealed horror. "Betty Haydon—stabbed to death in the Corona cinema. Last night, you say? It's fantastic. Like some ghastly nightmare. I can't believe it. It's so—so motiveless—"

"We don't think that, Mr. Kent. We think she may have known too much and that she had to be silenced. I am speaking, of course, from the point of view of the murderer. There is no doubt that the two victims died by the same hand."

"The Haydon girl," said Kent, half to himself. "Thin, sallow, very opinionated. She always argued over every correction I made to her drawings. She was Miss Garth's friend, I've seen them about together. Miss Garth—" he looked up anxiously, "will she be mixed up in this? Is she in any danger?"

"We are attending to that," said Collier with intentional vagueness. "In any case, whatever Betty may have known or suspected she did not tell her friend. I fancy she was rather enjoying the sense of power which her special knowledge—whatever it was—may have given her."

Kent nodded. "You are probably right. I got the idea that she resented being unnoticed. The new students have to go through that. Of course, if a girl is unusually pretty it's different."

"An inferiority complex, and this helped to even things up. If only she had come to us at once instead of hugging her secret," said Collier. "Well, there it is."

"Is there anything I can do?"

"Yes. I must speak to the students before they leave. Will you come with me?"

"Certainly."

They went first to the life classroom where a babble of conversation ceased abruptly as they entered. Collier stood by the door and made a short speech.

"I have to tell you that there has been another murder. One of your fellow students, Miss Betty Haydon, was stabbed last night in the balcony of the Corona picture house. So far we have no clue to the murder's identity, but it is possible that some of you may be able to help us. Did anyone here visit the Corona yesterday afternoon or evening?"

Nobody spoke or moved. He looked slowly round the semicircle of white shocked faces. "Was anyone here in Scanbridge?"

After a brief pause a young man answered huskily, "I was. My uncle and aunt live there. I went over by the six o'clock bus. They dine at seven. We played bridge afterwards until eleven. I stayed the night and came back here by the first bus."

"Thank you, Mr.—"

"Edmunds. Jack Edmunds."

"That's quite clear and satisfactory. And your uncle's name and address, just as a matter of form."

"The same as mine. The house is called The Firs. It's on the main road."

Collier waited a moment, but nobody else volunteered any account of their movements. He drew a long breath. There was something more that had to be said.

"I don't want to alarm you; but I have to ask you to face the fact that the murderer is at large. Not for long, I hope. We are doing our best. But meanwhile I want you all to be very careful. Don't go to the cinema, don't go for lonely walks, keep together as much as you can. Don't go out after nightfall. It can only be for a few days, perhaps only a few hours. That is all."

One of the girls said, "Are you giving us police protection?"

"I'm giving you good advice. You'll be safe while you keep together."

He had scarcely left the room with Kent when a babel of voices broke out.

Kent groaned. "This is the end. Every one whose home is at a distance will be off by the first train."

"That won't do." Collier turned back and re-opened the door.

"None of you to leave the district, please. Don't do it if you want to make a good impression. You're all under suspicion, remember."

"Oh, I say, Inspector, have a heart—"

"I mean it. Stay put. Let that be your contribution to our efforts."

Much the same scene was repeated in the preliminary classroom, but here the effect produced was even greater, for his hearers had worked in close proximity to the dead girl, and her easel stood where she had left it with a drawing half finished, pinned to her board. There were whispers of, "What about Cherry Garth? They were always together. Where's Cherry?"

Collier told them that the news had been broken to Miss Garth, and that she was too much upset to come to school.

There was more whispering and a sharp-faced girl called out, "You haven't arrested her, have you?"

"Certainly not." He repeated his warning.

His appeal had met with no response. Nobody in the preliminary class had gone to Scanbridge during the last twenty-four hours.

When they were in the corridor again he asked Kent if he could see the attendance book for the previous year.

Kent took him into the small, over-crowded office of the secretary and, after a brief search, unearthed the book under some old numbers of the *Studio*.

"You aren't very methodical here," remarked Collier.

"I know," said Kent ruefully. "It's a mess. I'm afraid Miss Roland didn't bother."

"Is that the secretary? How is it I haven't seen her?"

"She was away with a cold, and when her mother heard about the murder she wouldn't let her come back. I'm dealing with the correspondence *pro tem*, but there hasn't been any actually, except a bill for paints and canvas. We buy artists' materials, you see, and sell again to the students."

Collier was turning over the leaves of the attendance book.

"There was an Arnold Mansfield eighteen months ago," he said. "Would that be your nephew?"

"Yes. He was here for a couple of terms. He has a knack for quick sketches, but no perseverance. He was just playing about, so I advised him to try something else."

"What did he try?"

"I'm afraid I can't tell you. He was annoyed with me for turning him down here and he has not been very forthcoming since. I believe he has had various jobs, but I, don't know what they were."

"He was one of Althea Greville's admirers during the three weeks she spent here, wasn't he?"

Kent looked uncomfortable. "He hung round her. Yes. But there was nothing in it. There was a string of them. I believe they made up parties to drive to road houses or go to the cinema. There was no harm in it, though I'm afraid it made a good deal of talk in the village and unpleasantness at the time."

"I rather wonder that you booked her again."

"I wish to God I hadn't," said Kent violently. "But she seemed so down on her luck. I was sorry for her."

"She lodged with the Pearces on the previous occasion. Pearce told me so just now. Well, thank you, Mr. Kent. You'll be going home to your lunch, and there will be something ready for me at the Green Man, and my sergeant, I hope, waiting."

He found Duffield in their sitting-room, patiently eyeing a table laid for two.

"There's no bread by your plate," he said as he rang the bell.

"No. I've eaten it. I'd have started chewing the knives and forks if you'd been much longer. What a case! No sleep, and no breakfast to speak of," sighed Duffield. He brightened at the sight of a large and well-browned steak and kidney pie, accompanied by cabbage and roast potatoes.

"This is something like," he said buoyantly, as the pie was followed by a jam roly-poly. The landlady of the Green Man was a good plain cook. The stout sergeant heaved a sigh of repletion as he pushed back his chair. "It's been a morning," he said, "going through that picture house crowd. Two cleaners, three commissionaires, four usher-ettes, the young lady in the pay desk, to say nothing of the manager. Two of the girls had hysterics and the manager wasn't much better. He says they might as well close down, and I daresay he's right. They won't feel much like going to the pictures at Scanbridge while the killer is about."

"Did you get any sort of pointer?"

"Not a thing. If you ask me those girls would be too busy chattering about their boy friends to notice a murder being committed under their very noses, and they hardly get a chance to know their patrons by sight or to notice sinister strangers. You know how it is in cinemas. You go straight in through the vestibule, plank down your money, and the darkness swallows you up. If there's a queue the commissionaire is too busy throwing out his chest in his fancy uniform to notice its component parts. I really wonder more people aren't bumped off at the flicks."

"Did he follow her in, or did he know she always sat at the back of the balcony?" Collier pulled at his pipe. "Or—had they arranged to meet there? No, in that case she wouldn't have tried to persuade her friend Cherry Garth to go with her."

"Have you got anything?"

"Not really." After a moment he said slowly, "The betting is still on Morosini. He hasn't told me the truth about where he was last night. His story of a breakdown on the road is very unconvincing. He's engaged to Lady Violet Easedal. I saw her portrait in his London studio. A lovely thing. A man wouldn't want to lose her. Althea Greville might be the woman out of his past. Yes, one can imagine a motive. He could slip into the school unnoticed after the students had left. Betty Haydon might have seen him when she went back for her scarf. It must have been something like that. But was it Morosini? How would he know that she was in the balcony of the Corona? Someone must have followed her from here, or seen her in Scanbridge and gone in after her while it was still light; and he was in London then, having tea at the Ritz with his fiancée. That can be corroborated. He wasn't worrying about that."

"Suppose Betty rang him up at his London house and asked him to meet her to talk things over? Girls do silly things. She might want to make sure he couldn't give her some satisfactory explanation before she went to the police."

"You said yourself she wouldn't have asked the other girl to come with her if she was up to any funny business."

"I said that, but she might have felt the need of support," argued Collier. "She might have felt able to talk Cherry round. I got the impression that she had the stronger will, a bustling, managing type. The other is easy going, good natured. She would often give way rather than have a fuss."

"She didn't in this case," Duffield pointed out.

"No. Betty may have been in two minds about wanting her. We must try to find out if she put through a call to London. It would have to be before two when Morosini left his place. Make a note of that. We can't afford to neglect any point."

"You're sure in your own mind that he's the man?"

"No, I'm not. I'm far from sure." Collier got up and walked about the room. "I'm worried, Duff. This damned black-out. I'm afraid of what may happen in the dark. I've done all I could. I've got a man looking after the Garth girl. I've warned the others. Betty saw him when she went back for her scarf. Did he see her then, or did he learn later that she was a witness who must be silenced at any cost? She talked to her friend in the cottage where they had their lunch, with people coming in and out to get cigarettes from an automatic machine. I must talk to the woman who runs the place and find out if she overheard them and spread a rumour. There's Pearce. He's very bitter about Althea Greville. I don't altogether trust him."

"A bit past the age for making a fool of himself over a woman, isn't he?" said Duffield doubtfully.

His friend looked at him with a half smile. "Come, come, Sergeant, after all these years in the Force. There's no age limit. And his alibi isn't worth a row of beans. It depends on his wife and she would swear black was white for him. Why didn't she tell us Althea Greville lodged with them when she was down here last year? He may have fallen for her then. Poor Mrs. Pearce herself is about as glamorous as a pail of soapy water. Or there's young Mansfield. An unattractive cub, but we mustn't let that prejudice us. I learnt this morning that he was at the school last summer and was one of Althea's hangers on. Add to that he would know from Kent that she was working here again, and that from their house down the lane he could reach the school by crossing a couple of fields. But the motive is weak. She couldn't have been blackmailing him, for he hasn't a bean. She may have turned him down, but he's not the type to take that sort of trouble very hardly. His vanity would suffer, not his heart."

"Why couldn't it be Mr. Kent himself?" suggested Duffield.

Collier frowned. "Would he have re-engaged her if he felt like that about her?"

"He might if he was keen on her."

"Yes, I suppose so. We must keep his name on our list. Then the eight male members of the life class were here last year. You'd better tackle them all this afternoon, Duffield. Get signed statements of what they were doing about the time of the first killing, and yesterday. Luckily young men are gregarious. There ought to be plenty of corroborative evidence."

CHAPTER XI
SKETCHES IN THE MARGIN

CHERRY Garth, standing on the threshold of her sitting-room, looked up rather shyly at the large young man who occupied most of the space in the tiny passage between the umbrella stand and the foot of the stairs.

"I don't know how I'm to explain about you to Miss Tremlett without telling her everything and giving her a bad fright," she said.

P.C. Griffiths grinned. "She won't mind, miss, whatever. I'm walking out with her niece."

"Oh—that's all right then."

"Yes, miss. I'll just go into the kitchen and wait for her to come in. I know my way about. Doris and me have been more than once to tea with her auntie. You'll be quite safe with me within call. Don't go to the door, in any case. I'll attend to that."

"Very well. Did you tell the inspector about knowing Miss Tremlett?"

"No, miss. It don't do to shoot off your mouth when superior officers are about. They do the telling and we jump to it."

He grinned again and withdrew to the kitchen where she heard him stoking up the fire.

There was a gas fire in the front sitting-room for the lodger. Usually Cherry was. only at home in the evenings and on Sundays. She put a shilling in the slot of her meter, and, when she had lit the fire, drew up one of the shabby wicker armchairs and sank into it. She was shivering with cold, the result partly of delayed shock. This awful thing that had happened—she had not really taken it in. There was a war on, and perhaps, before it was over, they would all be killed, but somehow, that was different, that was impersonal, like an earthquake, or being struck by lightning. This—if the inspector was right it meant that someone—and possibly someone she knew—had killed Betty because of something that Betty had seen or heard when she went back to the school for her scarf, and that she herself was in danger because she might have been in Betty's confidence.

If only poor Betty had not been so fond of dramatising herself and making mysteries. She wanted to be noticed, to be important. Cherry, with more talent than her friend—though she was too humble-minded to realise it—found more satisfaction in her work and had no craving for popularity. Betty used to say that if she could not be loved she would be feared. Poor Betty, talking such rubbish in her high-pitched voice.

"I know more than you think, Cherry, about lots of people. I don't miss much, and I can put two and two together. No, I'm not going to tell you—"

Poor Betty, who, with all her faults and weaknesses, could be sympathetic and kind, dying alone in the dark while, on the screen, Fred Astaire was singing "The way you look to-night".

Cherry knew exactly where she must have been sitting. Betty, who had long sight, liked to get as far as possible away from the screen and she did not care to move about. She always made for the last row but one on the left of the balcony, and at the matinees, which were attended mostly by elderly people who did not want to climb stairs, they were often almost alone up there. Later it filled up, but you didn't really notice the other people even when they were shuffling and breathing and suppressing coughs all round you, not if you were as keen on the films as Betty had been.

No use sitting there doing nothing. Cherry had brought down some stockings to mend. No use getting panicky. After the inquest she would be safe. The inspector had said so. He was going to see that it was made quite clear that she knew nothing at all that would be likely to lead to the arrest of the murderer. Meanwhile she was being protected. She had a policeman all to herself. A nice boy, though she could not help feeling that his attitude was rather more unofficial than the inspector would have approved. Perhaps, though, she was doing him an injustice. The landlady had returned and she could hear the hum of voices in the kitchen. It was just as well that Miss Tremlett should not be upset or alarmed, and he seemed to be managing her very well.

She came in at one o'clock with a plate of cold beef and a dish of potatoes on a tray.

"I've brought you a slice off yesterday's joint, and you can have a bit of my treacle pudding presently if you like. Evan tells me you're staying home today on account of being a witness at the inquest on Miss Haydon tomorrow. He'll be spending the day here on duty like as it's handy for the railway station if he's called," she said importantly. "I said to him, I said, 'Well, I didn't hold at first with Doris walking out with a policeman, being in the millinery at Hartle and Strutt's and all, but when there's a spot of crime having somebody in the Force does let you in on the ground floor like.' Not that he's said much, not more than I heard when I was out from one and another. A regular oyster he is."

She paused for breath and stared curiously at her lodger. "Miss Haydon was that little, dark, sallow-faced thing who used to come in by train and wait for you at the gate?"

"Yes."

"You look poorly. You've quite lost your colour. Gave you a shock I daresay. When did you hear?"

"The detective from Scotland Yard who is in charge of the case came here just after you went out and told me."

"There now!" exclaimed Miss Tremlett with sharp annoyance. "Just my luck. Tell me all about it later. I must go back to my young man now."

An aroma of sizzling sausages indicated that P.C. Griffiths was to have something more tasty than cold beef. It was evident that the landlady was too pleasurably excited at having to entertain her niece's boy friend to think much about the reason for his presence in her house.

Cherry was not hungry, but she forced herself to eat. After Miss Tremlett had brought her a cup of tea and fetched away the tray she got her book on anatomy and sat down at the table to make drawings of arm muscles, and, when she tired of that, little pencil sketches from memory of a face, always the same face, in profile. She was so absorbed that she hardly noticed the knocking at the front door until she heard Evan Griffiths' heavy step in the passage. The sitting-room door was ajar—the lock was weak and it seldom remained shut—so that she heard every word of the ensuing colloquy.

"Oh—good afternoon—can I see Miss Garth?"

"I'm afraid not to-day, sir. Can you leave a message if you're a friend of hers?"

"I'd really like to see her, just for a few minutes. Is she—I suppose she's very upset. Naturally. My name is Kent—"

Cherry jumped up and went as far as the door of her sitting-room. That she went no farther was due to shyness and not to any recollection of Collier's warnings.

"Of course I can see Mr. Kent. Please ask him to come in."

The young Welshman scratched his head. "Indeed and whatever I don't know," he said doubtfully. "I have my orders—"

"Nonsense," said Cherry vigorously. She raised her voice. "Do please come in, Mr. Kent."

"Thank you very much."

Griffiths stood back reluctantly to allow him to pass in the narrow passage. He supposed it was all right. The young lady should know who were her friends. "Look here, miss," he compromised, "it'll be all right maybe if you leave your door open. I shan't be far off."

Kent followed Cherry into her little sitting-room.

"I felt I must come—" he said.

"Do please sit down. That chair is the most comfortable—"

"Thank you—"

There was an awkward pause. It was the first time they had met outside the school and on any terms but those of master and student. Kent, looking at her, felt as if he had never really seen her before. Hitherto she had always been overshadowed by her friend's stronger personality. He had not cared very much for Betty Haydon. She was too aggressive.

Cherry was thinking, "He's tired out. His face has got thinner in the last few days. Why is he taking it so hard? Why? It's horrible, but need he mind so much? I can't bear him to be so unhappy—"

He said, "That's a plain-clothes policeman, isn't it?"

"Yes. In case—you know about Betty?"

He nodded. "The inspector came to the school this morning to tell us. What a ghastly business. He seems to think she must have known—or at any rate guessed who killed Althea."

"Yes."

"You were her friend. She talked to you. Didn't she give you any hint?"

"I don't think so. I've been trying to remember. You know how it was?"

"Not exactly."

"We were the last out of school on Wednesday. It was a raw foggy afternoon and nobody had lingered, but Betty had dropped a new tube of crimson lake and we spent some time looking for it, and then, when we had got outside the gate, she realised that she had left her scarf in the cloakroom so she ran back to get it while I walked slowly on. I was nearly half-way here when she caught me up. She said, 'Well, well, well, I shall miss my train, but I've learnt something. Who would have thought it!' I said, 'Thought what? Don't talk in riddles,' but she only laughed and went on in the same way. 'I'm not one to tell tales out of school,' and that sort of thing. And then, the next day, when we weren't allowed in and the police were there, I said if she knew anything she ought to tell them, and she said she would think it over. Of course, we neither of us had the least idea that a murder had been committed, we thought it was something about the pilfering that has been going on this term."

"Oh, that," said Kent, as if this was a new point of view. "I remember now, Hollis told me some of the students had complained to him that odds and ends were taken from their lockers. Good Lord! You may have got something there, Miss Garth. Suppose the thief went into the life classroom, not knowing that Althea was still there—she would be behind the screen, dressing—if she caught him in the act he might have turned on her—"

"I suppose so," said Cherry doubtfully. "That would mean that it's one of the students. I once read in a book on famous crimes that murderers have very bright eyes. I wonder if that's true."

"I should hardly think so," said Kent. "I fancy there are no outward signs. I see you have been working at arm muscles. These sketches aren't bad. You've got a good line. Do you want to go in for illustrating?"

He had glanced at the rows of little pencilled heads on the margin of her anatomical drawing book without appearing to be aware that she had been sketching his own profile from memory, but poor Cherry was crimson with embarrassment. Had he recognised himself, or hadn't he? And, if he had, what must he think?

She said, "Yes. I'm always trying to catch a likeness. I do everybody."

"You've got talent. You ought to be in the life class next term—if there is a next term."

"Oh—what do you mean?"

"You must know that the school is going down, and what with the war and this business—"

"Oh dear—"

He looked at her. "Should you mind very much? Honestly, you could learn as much at any good municipal art school. The fees here are absurdly high."

She was thinking, "He's guessed that I'm in love with him. I've given myself away. Those sketches. He's trying to tell me it's no use and that I'd better go away."

She heard herself saying in a strained voice "If you think that—all right. I won't come back next term."

He said, "I may not be here myself. If they won't take me in the army I may get some form of war work." He got up from his chair. "So you can't help the police at all. Betty

Haydon lived with her aunt, didn't she? Would she have talked more freely to her?"

"I don't think so. They weren't very pally. Miss Haydon has her own interests, church work and social work. Betty was more likely to say something to old Emma. That's her aunt's maid. She's been with them for years. If I were the inspector I'd try her. He might get something."

"He probably will if he hasn't already. Well, I must be getting along."

"Thank you for coming."

She watched him from the window, get on to the bicycle he had left by the gate and pedal up the road to the village. Her face was still burning and her feet and hands were cold. The net result of his visit was to leave her feeling more miserable than ever. Her landlady, bustling in a little later, found her sitting over the gas fire.

"I thought you might be asking Mr. Kent to stop for a cup of tea. I was getting out one of my best cloths in case."

Cherry had thought of it, but her courage had failed her.

Miss Tremlett talked on. "They're saying in the village that he was sweet on that young woman that was done in at the school. No better than she should be by all accounts, but men are funny that way. Well, it's lucky I made a large fruit cake, with Evan here, and my mother's brother came along just now with some greens from his allotment, so he's stopping, too. No, he isn't neither, for there's the back gate, and it's time I oiled those hinges. I'll bring your tea as soon as the water boils, miss. You'll feel better when you've had a cup."

CHAPTER XII
THE POWERS OF DARKNESS

THE flat, in a new block in a side street on the north side of the Park, had an automatic lift and no porter, and was altogether not nearly so resplendent as Collier had expected. The door was opened by a plain-faced and thick-set young woman wearing slacks of a startling shade of magenta that matched her lipstick.

Collier asked for Lady Violet Easedal.

"She's just going out."

"I shall not keep her long."

"What is your business? I can't have her worried," said the young woman belligerently.

Collier smiled. He had placed her now. This was the friend to whom Morosini had referred. He produced his official card.

"You may have read of the tragic affair at the Morosini school. I understand that Lady Violet lunched with Mr. Morosini yesterday. I have one or two questions to ask her, purely formal, a matter of routine."

"You'd better come in. I'll tell her. Sit down, and smoke if you want to. I'm Susan Little."

Miss Little was noticeably more friendly. Collier, who had some experience of the type, could guess how her jealous possessive affection for the other girl had been wounded by the latter's engagement. Anything that would damage Morosini in the eyes of his fiancée would have the collaboration of Miss Little.

The living-room in which she had left him was furnished mainly with cushions and ash trays. There was a radiogram in one corner. The only picture on the walls was a masterly sketch in oils of a girl's head. Collier was still gazing at it when the original came in.

"Not bad, is it," she said casually.

He smiled. "I should call that an understatement."

She was dressed for the street in a black coat with a fur collar. Her golden hair gleamed under the brim of her small black hat. She was as beautiful, but perhaps not as lovely as her pictures. It was a fine distinction. Collier made it as he realised that in spite of her apparent carelessness her blue eyes were hard and aware.

"Susan says you want to talk to me about Aldo. I can't imagine why."

"You lunched with Mr. Morosini at the Ritz yesterday."

"No. He called for me here about half-past two. We walked through the Park and had tea at the Ritz. I had to go on duty at the canteen at six so I came home in a taxi."

"You left him then outside the Ritz. At what hour?"

"About four or soon after. He was driving out to Elder Green."

"Did he tell you anything of the trouble at the school?"

"I asked him. We had seen a short account in the paper. He didn't want to talk about it. He was very upset, naturally."

"He was in a hurry to get back," suggested Collier.

"I wouldn't say that. His servant had told him the police had been to Bello Sguardo. He rather resented that. His point was that he knew absolutely nothing about it all and he didn't see why he should be dragged into it."

"You agreed with that view?"

She lit a cigarette and flicked the match into the fireplace. "I sympathised. He's Italian, you know, and a genius, and very temperamental. You needn't sniff, Susan."

"Sorry," said Miss Little. "He's upset. That's his angle, and nothing else matters."

"You're always so damnably unfair about Aldo."

They glared at each other and Collier thought it politic to intervene. "Have you heard from him to-day?"

"He rang me up this morning. He always does if we aren't meeting. Why?"

"He told you about his misadventure?"

"You mean about the car breaking down? Perfectly foul for him."

"What was that, Vi?" asked Miss Little curiously.

"Something went wrong with the engine and he was stuck by the roadside for hours and hours, the poor sweet."

"Really," said Miss Little, "and couldn't he do anything? I always think the main roads in the home counties are lousy with motor repair shops."

"I understand that in the course of time a lorry driver offered his services and put the matter right," said Collier smoothly. "Mr. Morosini himself isn't very good with engines."

Miss Little opened her mouth and shut it again without saying anything. Lady Violet murmured, "The poor sweet—" rubbed out the end of her cigarette in an ash tray and produced a mirror and a lipstick from her bag. "I'm sorry. I shall have to rush—"

"It has been very good of you to grant me this interview," said Collier formally. "Good afternoon. I can let myself out." He went down by the stairs, crossed the road, and waited in a doorway until he had seen Lady Violet come out, walk down the road and get on to a bus. Then he went back to the flat and rang the bell. The door was opened by Miss Little.

"I must apologise," he said. "I'm afraid I left my gloves. Very careless of me—"

Without a word she went into the living-room and came back with the gloves. Her beady eyes met his steadily as she gave them to him.

"Is that all?"

"Well—you don't like Mr. Morosini much, do you?"

"I like his work. But he's not good enough for Vi. Apart from his work he's rotten."

"But she's in love with him."

"Pah!" said Miss Little. "Her people don't know how to handle her. It would have petered out before this if they hadn't opposed it. Her brother came here and called him a Wop and an outsider, and made her feel that by sticking to him she was being broad-minded and intelligent and all that. You'd better come in, hadn't you? We may as well have this out. It's my flat actually. Vi. came to me after the blazing row she had with her parents over her precious Aldo. Mind you," she added, with reluctant honesty, when he had followed her into the living-room, "he's attractive. Got oodles of S.A. I've felt it myself, though he's never bothered to exert his charm on me."

She squatted, cross-legged, on a cushion and lit a cigarette. "Sit down, won't you—"

Collier, after some hesitation, chose the window-sill.

"I thought you were going to say something just now, before Lady Violet went out, and that you changed your mind. I wonder why—"

"That was sharp of you," she said, "but, of course, you would be. I mean, they don't promote the stodgy, insensitive type, do they? It was just—what made you say he wasn't any good with machinery?"

"He told me so himself."

"Really? That's very unlike him. I've heard him boast that he can do anything with a car. He goes in for being versatile, like that earlier, but, of course, very inferior artist, Leonardo da Vinci."

Collier laughed in spite of himself. "You're a hard hitter, Miss Little."

She grinned. "Let's come to the point. You think he's lying about that breakdown, don't you?"

"I don't say that, but I'd like some corroborative evidence. We shall try to get the lorry driver, but if he does not turn up we shan't be much better off."

She was frowning as she ground the stub of her cigarette into an ash tray. "Why is it important?"

He decided that it could do no harm to tell her what everyone would know before long. "There was another murder yesterday evening. A girl was found stabbed in a Scanbridge cinema. She was one of Mr. Morosini's students. There will be some account of it in the evening papers."

Her jaw dropped. "Good Lord! You don't really think he—" her broad face flushed a dull, unbecoming red. "I don't believe it," she said violently. "You can't pin it on him. It's ridiculous. Why shouldn't his breakdown be genuine? In the black-out he couldn't see to mess round with the carburettor and things. And you come snooping round here trying to entrap me into saying things I don't really mean. I—" she swallowed hard. "Do you mind going now?"

He got up at once. "I'm sorry I upset you. Don't worry, Miss Little. We don't arrest people without pretty good evidence."

He wondered as he left the block of flats for the second time if his afternoon was being entirely wasted. It was evident that he would get no further help from Lady Violet or her friend. He was still convinced that Morosini had lied to him, and that, wherever he had spent the time when he was not actually driving between the Ritz hotel and his house at Elder Green, it had not been sitting in his car by the roadside.

He caught a bus to Westminster. There would be just time to report to his superintendent. Cardew was in his office, enmeshed, like a stout spider, in a web of forms. He laid down his pen with a sigh of relief as Collier came in.

"All this writing," he grumbled. "How are you getting on?"

"Not at all," said Collier dejectedly.

"This second murder ought to help you to get your man. Have you tabulated the points that are common to both crimes? It should be possible to cross off several of your former suspects."

"Yes, sir."

Cardew looked at him. "Well, isn't it?"

"I'm pretty sure of one thing, and that is that the same person is responsible for both killings."

"Is that all?"

"Pretty nearly."

Cardew picked up the receiver of the house telephone on his desk and asked for a pot of tea for two, with biscuits, to be sent up from the canteen. "You were up all last night, I suppose?"

"Yes. The sergeant and I were just about to turn in when they rang us up from the cinema where the girl's body had been found."

"And what have you done since?"

Cardew listened without interruptions to Collier's account of that day's activities. The tea was brought in and he filled both cups.

Collier drank his eagerly. It was hot and strong. "So you see how it is, sir. The black-out makes it impossible for us to keep tabs on anyone after dark. Kent, Morosini, Pearce, the caretaker, or—for matter of that, Mrs. Pearce—any of the students might have been there and have got away unseen after doing the job. I think the motive for the second murder is clear. The killer must have been seen by Betty Haydon when she went back to the cloakroom for her scarf. It's a wonder he didn't silence her then and there, but perhaps he only caught a glimpse of her, only heard retreating footsteps and the closing of a door."

"You have a theory that she wrote to him and suggested a meeting in Scanbridge?"

"Wrote, or, more likely, telephoned. It would be in keeping with her character, I think. She was an ordinary-looking girl who had never had any excitement or power over anyone. I gathered from what her friend Cherry Garth said that she thought the whole thing very thrilling. She evidently didn't realise the danger."

"Something may turn up," said Cardew, after a pause. "I don't expect miracles, and neither does the A.C. I hope. The inquests are to-morrow, aren't they. They'll both be adjourned, of course. If you take my advice you'll turn in early to-night. You're too tired to see things in their right proportions at present. It certainly is a case with many possibilities. It'll be a feather in your cap if you clear it up."

"Who would be your choice, sir, if I may ask? I've tried to make my report as objective as I can and not to impart my own likes and dislikes."

Cardew smiled good-humouredly. "You may have tried, but I can always see through you." He took out his pouch and filled his pipe. "In your place," he said deliberately, "I would pay rather more attention than you seem to have done hitherto to that young fellow, Kent's nephew. What's his name—Arnold Mansfield."

"I'll tackle him next, sir."

In the train going down to Scanbridge, Collier's fellow travellers were reading about the cinema murder in the evening papers.

Collier had bought an *Evening Post* and he read the opening sentences of an article by a special correspondent.

"There is a killer abroad in the streets of this little quiet market town, and the people are panic stricken. Mothers are afraid to allow their children out of doors. A woman said to me—"

"Blah!" thought Collier angrily, and yet there was some truth in it. Was there anything he had left undone? Could the death of Betty Haydon be laid at his door? Was he responsible through some piece of carelessness? He had never liked the case from the first. There was something about it that reminded him of that horrible shapeless mass Peer Gynt had met on the road that could not be handled or removed. The Boyg, wasn't it? He roused himself with a start, realising that he had begun to doze and that the train was slowing down. It was so easy to pass one's station in the black-out. The black-out. The powers of darkness. He jumped down after the others, leaving his crumpled paper on the seat, gave up his ticket to a collector who was too busy verifying seasons to lift his eyes from the tiny circle of dim light in which he scrutinised them, and melted into the shadows of the station yard where the shaded head-lamps of the waiting taxis were like the eyes of predatory beasts in the night of the jungle. He was just in time to catch the bus to Elder Green.

The bus stopped frequently for passengers to get on or off. It was too dark to see their faces as they and the conductor fumbled anxiously over their change.

"Put me down at Mill Lane."

"Is this the Wheatsheaf?"

"Don't let me pass my turning."

Collier's feet grew colder and colder as the clumsy vehicle rattled along the winding lanes.

"Surely this is a very roundabout way to Elder Green?"

"That's right, sir," said the conductor, "but we have to touch as many of the smaller villages as we can. Why, if you go on foot and know all the short cuts across the fields it isn't much over four miles from Scanbridge to Elder Green, while it's nine by the bus route. But most people takes the bus if they haven't got cars or bikes. Walking's gone out except for them hikers, and they has to dress up for it seemingly. My old grandmother was the postwoman and covered twenty-five miles every day, and she didn't need no shorts neither. Here you are, sir, unless you want the other end of the village. We don't stop in between."

Collier got out and felt his way along by the house-walls to a remembered landmark, the old stone mounting block by the door of the Green Man.

Duffield was in their sitting-room enjoying a sit-down tea which appeared to include sausages and a blackberry tart.

"I hope you don't mind me beginning without you. I waited until six."

Collier drew up his chair. "Don't apologise. Any news?"

"I spent the afternoon at the school putting those life class students through it. They've all got pretty good alibis for yesterday evening."

"That's a comfort," mumbled Collier, with his mouth full. "I'm going round to Poona presently."

"Mr. Kent again?"

"No. The nephew."

"Him," said Duffield with distaste. "The landlord was telling me about him. He and his mother stayed here before they moved into their house, and he was glad when they went. The young chap was always pestering the barmaid they had then; a nice respectable young woman who wouldn't have anything to do with him; and his ma wanted a lot of waiting on. He says he's sorry for Mr. Kent, such a nice quiet gentleman and gave no trouble at all."

"I like Kent myself," said Collier, "but we must not be led away by these natural affinities. Lots of people liked Crippen. He, too, was nice and quiet and gave no trouble."

The sergeant looked up quickly. "I've wondered about him. Mr. Kent, I mean. He could have—"

"So could at least four other people. Suspects reduced to five. That's not bad considering that we began with fifty." He struggled into his overcoat. "Stay here until I come back, Duffield. I shan't be long. After that, if nothing more breaks, we'll call it a day."

He was wondering, as he splashed through the puddles and stumbled over the ruts in the lane, why he had thought himself fortunate to be promoted to the C.I.D. He thought yearningly of men who went home every day from the office by the same train and spent their evenings arranging their collection of postage stamps or playing bridge with the wife and a couple of friends. Bridge. The Mansfields, mother and son, were bridge fiends. His mind, which had run momentarily on to a side line, was switched back on to the main track. He found the gate of Poona, after some fumbling. There was a crack of light showing in the ground floor window on the right of the door where the curtain had been carelessly drawn. He rang the bell, and after an interval, heard heavy steps coming down the passage, and a woman's voice spoke through the letter box.

"Who is it?"

"Inspector Collier, Mrs. Mansfield."

"My brother is out, if it's him you want."

"I'd like a few words with you, please."

"Oh—very well."

She opened the door and moved back to allow him to pass in. "This ridiculous black-out," she said irritably. "You'd better come in here."

He followed her into the shabby dining-room where he had talked with Kent. "I'm sorry he's out," he said pleasantly. "I suppose I've just missed him."

"No. He hasn't been in since lunch. I should have been out too. Arnold and I go to the Winnington Smiths once a week for bridge, but they rang up to say she is starting a cold. What can I do for you, Inspector?" She was a stout woman, with greasy black hair very fashionably dressed, and a broad red face toned down by a liberal coating of powder to a pale shade of mauve. Her hard eyes met his warily. She had not asked him to sit down.

"Perhaps I could see your son?"

"He is out, too."

"Bad luck. When will he be home?"

"I have no idea."

"Has he been out since lunch, too?"

"As a matter of fact he has. He did not tell me where he was going, but he may have run up to Town. He wants to go on the films, and he has put his name down at the agencies. He may have heard of something."

"He has tried several things, hasn't he?"

"He has a great deal of talent," said his mother defensively. "What I say is you can't tell what really suits you until you have tried. He's not a plodder like John, but he's brilliant. I tell John it's all very well for him, but you can't harness a racehorse to a cab."

"He attended the Morosini school for a couple of terms?"

"Yes. But he said to me, 'Mother, I've got it in me, but they're killing it. Mr. Hollis and Uncle John. They simply don't understand. Mine is a delicate individual art, and they're trying to iron it out.' It was worse than useless for him to go on there."

Collier suppressed a smile. Morosini was a poseur, and here, it seemed, was another. "I suppose," he said, "they wanted him to draw accurately and all that."

"Exactly." She forgot her enmity, warmed by his understanding. "Do sit down, Mr.—er—As he said, 'I draw it as I see it.' But if he can only get a hearing I'm sure he will be a success as a film actor. When I saw that young man they make such a fuss about last week—Robert Taylor—I said to myself, 'Well, really'."

"Did you go to *Swing Time* at the Corona?"

"No. I don't really go often. I have so many bridge engagements. Arnold may have been."

She answered so easily that he realised that she had not heard of the second murder. Poona was not on the telephone, and if she had not been out it was understandable. Kent might have told her at lunch, but perhaps he dreaded her comments, and her son, if he knew, might have his own reasons for saying nothing about it. He said, picking his words carefully, "I haven't had a chat with your son yet, and it's my job to talk to everybody, you know. People sometimes hold valuable clues and don't know it themselves. When he comes in would you ask him to come and see me at the Green Man any time this evening or to-morrow morning up to nine o'clock. I have to attend the inquest later."

"Really, I don't see why he should be worried," she said with a return to her former acid manner. "He knows nothing whatever about the case."

"I understand that he went about with Althea Greville when she was posing for the life class rather more than a year ago," said Collier quietly. He saw that he had given her a shock. Her high colour faded. She looked afraid. But she answered quickly.

"I am sure you are mistaken. There is a great deal of gossip in villages. You must not believe everything you hear. Arnold is a good-looking boy. Girls run after him. It's not his fault. He dislikes it intensely, but he can't help it."

"Oh yeah!" thought Collier, as he trudged back along the lane to the Green Man. He had repeated his request that young Mansfield should come to see him, and Mrs. Mansfield had agreed, though very ungraciously, to give Arnold his message.

He would take off his boots and sit by the fire writing his report. But it was not to be. Duffield met him at the door of their sitting-room. The stolid sergeant was more moved than Collier had ever seen him.

"'I've just been rung up," he said. "Thank God you're back, sir. We've got to be quick—"

CHAPTER XIII
A KNOCK AT THE DOOR

MISS Haydon had gone, as usual, to evensong at the Abbey. She was due to play the piano afterwards at a Girl Guides' Social. Emma had suggested that she should ring up the vicar and ask him to find a substitute, but Miss Haydon would not hear of it.

"I shall carry on," she said. "I am sure Betty would have wished it."

Emma sniffed. She knew that Betty's unconcealed indifference to the Girl Guide movement had always been a source of annoyance to her aunt, but it was no use saying so now. Miss Haydon had done her duty by her orphaned niece, but the two had never got on very well together, and though the old lady was deeply shocked by Betty's tragic end, Emma, who knew them both, was too much of a realist to expect her to be overcome with grief.

"I shall miss poor Miss Betty more than she does," she thought, as she sat down by her kitchen fire with a basket of stockings to mend. She was alone in the house but for Tommy, her black cat, who was curled up, purring, on the hearthrug at her feet. No fuss about screening the windows to-night, for the blinds had been drawn all day. During the afternoon wreaths had been arriving, and they had been placed in Betty's room. The funeral was to take place the next day, after the inquest. Miss Haydon had rung up Messon and Jebb's, the big firm in Scanbridge, and they were making all the arrangements.

"Something young about the house," thought Emma. "She used to come down here most evenings to talk to me. Poor Miss Betty and, her film stars, and me always hoping she'd take up with a real boy some day. A pity she was so fond of snooping. 'Knowledge is power,' she used to say, and I used to tell her 'If you want to be liked, miss, don't you be a Poll Pry,' but she only laughed at me." She sighed as she threaded her needle, and then her heart seemed to miss a beat as she realised that she was mending a ladder in a stocking that would never be worn again by its owner. She knew that Miss Haydon would leave to her the dreary business of looking over the dead girl's clothes. All those pictures cut out of film magazines and pinned up on the walls in her bedroom would have to be taken down and burnt with the rather smudgy and amateurish drawings and the smeared studies in oils that she had brought home at intervals from the Morosini school.

"I can't credit it, somehow," said Emma aloud, "seems as if I'd be hearing her key turn in the lock any minute—"

The house, built in the reign of Queen Anne, of mellow red brick, with a flight of steps leading up to the front door, and a white pillared portico, was one of a row, but was divided from its neighbour on the right by a narrow passage leading to an alley at the back which was used by the tradespeople and was also a short cut down the hill to the station. The basement was reached by a flight of steps into the area shut off from the pavement by iron railings and a gate. Emma, from her kitchen window, saw nothing of the passers-by but their feet.

There was another door opening out of the scullery into the side alley, but it was only used once in six weeks when the men brought the coal.

Emma was putting away her work-basket when she noticed the knocking. The old house was so still at night that the least sound was audible, the ticking of the grandfather clock in the hall, the fall of ashes in the kitchen grate, the crackling of her starched apron as she moved. At first she thought it might be a tap dripping in the scullery sink, and then, as she listened, she knew that it was someone rapping very softly and furtively on the side door.

It was warm and cosy in the lamp-lit and fire-lit kitchen, a focus of heat and light surrounded by dank black cells. Emma, who scorned modern amenities, had to light a candle to visit the larder, the wash-house, or the coal cellar after dark.

"Bother," she said as she struck a match and held it to the wick. She was not afraid—but who could be knocking at the side door at this hour? Her friend, the maid at number thirty, sometimes dropped in for a gossip and a cup of cocoa, but she would come down the area steps, and, in any case, she was nervous, and was not likely to turn up until after the funeral.

"I don't know as I blame her," thought Emma. "There's death in the house, or as good as." She had shut the door of the spare room which was filled with wreaths, but the acrid scent of chrysanthemums was everywhere.

The knocking, which had ceased for a minute, had begun again.

"All right," she said impatiently. "I'm coming—"

She passed through the scullery and the short passage leading out of it with the doors of the coal cellar and the long disused wine cellar on either side, and stooped to draw the lower bolt. Her eyes were sore with crying and her head ached. Poor little Miss Betty. She opened the door and the draught blew out her candle. Less than a minute later the front door bell rang.

Miss Haydon sat in her usual place in the nave throughout the service of evensong. She had not been very fond of her niece, but she was sincerely shocked by the tragedy of her death. She did not want to think about it. A horrible sordid affair. She had never approved of Betty going to the cinema as she did, but it was no use trying to control these modern young people, and Betty had always gone her own way. She was thoroughly upset, her thoughts wandered while the psalms were being sung, and even while Canon Strutt was reading the lesson in his beautiful voice. Miss Haydon would have been much offended if she had been told that the thrill she experienced when the Canon intoned the Amen was not dissimilar to Betty's when she watched the dancing of Mr. Fred Astaire. Several people spoke to her on her way out, and the Canon's wife caught up with her just as she reached the black-out screen by the door into the cloisters.

"My dear Miss Haydon, we are so truly sorry for you. That poor girl. A horrifying business. Most alarming. The Canon said at once that it must be the work of a maniac. A maniac at large. Indeed, I was quite surprised to see so many in the congregation to-night. It was very brave of you to come. We feared you would be prostrate—"

Mrs. Strutt, who did not really like Miss Haydon, spoke with more than usual warmth in a well-meant effort to show her sympathy.

Miss Haydon, who always felt it was rather a pity that the Canon had married at all, answered stiffly that she felt it was a duty to carry on, and that she was due at the Girl Guides' Social.

"That is the spirit," said Mrs. Strutt, "though I'm afraid we shouldn't all be so wonderful. But that's one reason why I wanted to get hold of you—it really makes things rather difficult you not being on the phone—the point is that the Social is cancelled. We called a committee meeting and decided that, under the circumstances, the girls would be better at home. We must not take any unnecessary risks. I've strict injunctions to wait for the Canon to join me now," she added with a little laugh. "He won't trust me alone even just across the Close. And what about you, Miss Haydon? Isn't there anybody going your way?"

"I'm in no danger," said Miss Haydon curtly. "Good night, Mrs. Strutt. Thank you both for the beautiful wreath. It arrived just before I came out."

The other women had gone off in twos and threes but she went out alone. The wind met her and dashed a splatter of rain into her face. The branches of the elms creaked overhead. She had been a regular attendant at the Cathedral services for many years. It would be strange if she could not find her way home in the dark. And as to danger—she had accepted the fact of her niece's death by violence, but had not given any thought to the motive for the crime. She was a member of the committee. They had no right to call a meeting without informing her. It was not the first time she had been slighted. There was a subversive element, a tendency among the younger women to pamper the children. She and Mrs. Strutt never saw eye to eye. She sometimes wondered if the Canon regretted his marriage. He would be too loyal, of course, to admit it. There was a line of light there under a blind carelessly drawn. Miss Haydon wondered if she should warn the occupants, and decided to leave it to the air raid warden.

The other houses in the terrace were all in darkness, even number fifteen, where there were several noisy girls and young men of whom she did not approve. She had always been afraid that Betty would make friends with them, regardless of the fact that the father was in trade. Their wireless was turned on full blast as usual. Miss Haydon sighed as she felt her way along the railings to her own front door and fitted her latchkey in the lock. The wireless programme had often been a source of dissension between her and her niece.

A night light was burning in a basin on the hall table and its tiny flame was a dim little oasis in a sea of darkness. The heavy perfume of the wreaths drifted down the stairs. Miss Haydon set her umbrella in the hall stand and slipped off her goloshes.

"Emma!"

It was unlike Emma not to be ready for her. The old woman usually called out, "Is that you'm?" as she closed the front door. By this time she should have been lumbering up the steep flight of stairs from the basement with the supper tray.

"Emma. I've come in—"

There was no answer.

Miss Haydon went to the top of the stairs and peered down. A light was burning in the kitchen, but there was no sound or movement. Miss Haydon seldom visited the basement, and she had disapproved of Betty's running down to gossip with the old servant. She would not have gone down now if she had not fancied that she noticed a smell of scorching.

Emma, she supposed, must have gone up to her bedroom and left the saucepan of bread and milk on the stove. She hurried down and was just in time to save it from boiling over.

"Very careless," she said sharply, as she turned the steaming mess into the cup on the tray. She would have to speak to Emma. This was no time to be buying new saucepans. And what was the use of keeping up a large fire if the door into the scullery and those draughty unused offices was left open? She went to close it and met a clammy breath of cold air that puzzled her and revived a long buried memory of going down to the cellar with Papa to fetch a bottle of wine, one of the last of the vintage ports laid down by grandpapa. She moved forward, and something rolled away as her foot touched it. She glanced down, and, in the light from the open kitchen door saw the shattered fragments of a white china candlestick, and the candle itself which she had kicked aside. Emma's candlestick.

Miss Haydon was not imaginative, but in that moment the silence of the house took on some quality of horror. She knew that Emma kept an electric torch on the mantelpiece. She went back into the kitchen and fetched it. She was not a coward, and it did not occur to her to rush upstairs and go for help. If there was anything wrong she would find it out for herself. Nothing amiss in the scullery. Emma's tea-cloths hung on the line, the brick floor had been scrubbed, the potatoes for to-morrow's dinner had been peeled and left in water. But in the passage the door of the wine cellar had swung back on rusty hinges and, the ray from the torch, moving uncertainly, because Miss Haydon's hand had begun to shake, passed over a white face, and a crumpled apron that had once been white, lying at the foot of the cellar steps.

CHAPTER XIV
THE THIRD VICTIM

WHEN Collier and Duffield arrived the local superintendent met them in the hall.

"She's just been taken off in the ambulance to the Cottage Hospital. The doctor went with her, but you'll be able to see him later."

"Will she live?"

"I don't know. He wouldn't say. A fractured arm and head injuries. She was thrown down the cellar steps."

"You are sure of that? It couldn't have been an accident?"

"Miss Haydon tells us the wine cellar was never used. The door was not locked, but it had not been opened for years. It is close to a side door only used for bringing in coal, that gives on to an alley that connects the terrace with Tappit's Lane. That door should have been bolted, but it wasn't, and there are muddy foot-marks on the threshold and on the brick pavement."

"Clear enough to be of any use?"

"I'm afraid not. Just muddy smears."

"I'll have a look at them presently."

"We rang up the Scanbridge police and asked them to get in touch with you because this seemed to tie up with the Morosini school murder."

"Yes. I'm obliged to you, Superintendent. I'll be glad if we can work together, though I hope you mean to handle the case. My hands are full as it is. But if this woman's assailant was the murderer of Althea Greville and Betty

Haydon, we ought to be able to catch him between us. If only she recovers enough to furnish a description. But she may not have seen him—"

"We may get something from Miss Haydon," said the superintendent. "She's in the dining-room if you'll come this way. I was waiting for you—"

An hour and a half had passed since Miss Haydon had found Emma lying unconscious at the foot of the cellar stairs and she had recovered from the initial shock and regained her normal dry composure of manner. She recognised Collier.

"You are the policeman who came before about poor Betty. Please sit down, both of you. I am quite prepared to answer questions."

"Thank you. We should like to ascertain the time when the assault was committed as far as possible," began the superintendent.

"Did you see Miss Price before you went out this evening?"

"Yes. She had just answered the door to take in some flowers. I left her in the hall. That would be about twenty past six. Evensong was over at a quarter-past seven. Mrs. Strutt spoke to me on my way out but did not detain me. I was home by half-past seven."

"Has Emma Price any relatives or friends who are in the habit of visiting her about that hour?"

"Certainly not. I should not allow it. The maid at number thirty comes, but only very occasionally. Emma is not a native of Scanminster. She has a nephew living in London. I am afraid he is rather unsatisfactory and she has to help him at times, but he has never been here to my knowledge."

"I had better have his name and address."

"I can't help you there."

"Have you had any trouble lately with hawkers coming to the door and pestering you to buy their wares?"

"There was a man about a week ago who became abusive. I was upstairs but I heard him shouting. Emma got rid of him. She won't put up with any nonsense."

"You didn't see him? You can't describe him?"

"No. But I heard him saying something about getting even with her, and some very bad language. Surely you don't think—"

"We have to consider every possibility in a case like this," said the superintendent. "I think we had better have a look round her room before we go."

"Is that really necessary?"

"I think so. Have you any friends to whom you can go to-night, ma'am?"

But Miss Haydon disliked the idea of being turned out of her own house and said so in no uncertain terms.

She declared that she was not at all nervous, but agreed to a constable being left on guard in the basement. She had, she said, a gas ring in her bedroom and could make herself a cup of tea, and in the morning she could get a woman to come in daily, a most reliable person, the mother of one of her Girl Guides.

"Hard as nails," said the superintendent, when they had left her and were on their way up to Emma's bedroom on the top floor. "Doesn't care if the poor old woman lives or dies so long as she can get an adequate substitute."

"It's a type," said Collier. "Oddly enough, they often get better servants than more considerate employers."

Emma's room gave point to their comments, but the shabby chest of drawers and washstand were highly polished and the bare boards scrubbed white. A tiny strip of faded carpet lay beside the iron bedstead. There were two framed photographs on the chest of drawers, one a snapshot of her employer's niece, the dead girl, Betty Haydon, and another of a young man, not bad-looking, but with a slack mouth and an air of being a shade too pleased with himself.

The superintendent looked through the drawers. Neatly folded garments smelling of moth balls, a Bible, *Old Moore's Almanack*, a book of dreams, and a little bundle of letters. He glanced at one or two.

"Cadging appeals to dear Auntie, signed your loving nephew Cyril Wood," he remarked. "An address in Pimlico."

"We'll look up Cyril," said Collier, seeing that this was expected of him. He knew that the superintendent was right, and that the attack on Emma might prove to have nothing whatever to do with the murders at Elder Green and Scanbridge, in which case he was simply wasting his time. On the other hand, he had quickly seen that if Betty Haydon had been silenced because of what she knew the same motive might operate in the case of the old servant. He had learned from Miss Haydon that Betty, in spite of her aunt's disapproval, spent a good deal of time in the kitchen gossiping with Emma, a fact that might have become known to the murderer.

He looked at his watch. "I ought to push on to the hospital now," he said, "it's getting late. You know my phone number, The Green Man, Elder Green, if there are any fresh developments. What about the railway station and the local bus office? If the loving nephew is your man he might be going back to London."

"Leave all that to us," said the superintendent largely, "in a place of this size strangers are noticed."

Collier had left Duffield downstairs to pick up what he could. The sergeant joined him in the hall and they left the house together by way of the basement. Collier spent a few minutes inspecting the pavement of the alley outside the side door with the aid of his torch. The alley was under cover where it passed under the terrace and there were numerous muddy footmarks where people had walked through, but he found no trace of bicycle tyres. This was explained when he found a post at the end which would prevent any bicycle from coming through. Collier swore gently and led the way back to their waiting car, a battered Ford belonging to the landlord of the Green Man.

"What's your idea, Inspector?" ventured Duffield, as they nosed their way through the narrow winding streets of the little hill town following the dim blue light of their screened headlamps.

"Two of our suspects are cyclists and live about seven miles away. Is this the hospital entrance?"

The porter, after, some parleying, showed them into a waiting-room. A Sister came to them presently. The police surgeon had gone home. There was nothing more he could do. The arm had been set and the patient made comfortable for the night. No, she had not regained consciousness. She might do so at any time. Yes, she was on the danger list. She agreed, reluctantly, that a constable might be allowed to be within hearing, behind a screen, and Collier was permitted to use the telephone to make the necessary arrangements with the local police headquarters.

Collier's next and last visit was to the railway station at the foot of the hill. There, after studying the timetable, he interviewed the station master and a ruddy-faced youth who combined the duties of porter and ticket-collector, and made certain arrangements for the following day.

The Town Hall at Scanbridge was a late seventeenth-century building of fine mellowed red brick, with a bust of Charles II, his ironic features framed by a very curly wig, observing his lieges in the Market Square from a niche over the main entrance.

Cherry Garth was brought from her lodgings in a police car and taken directly into a waiting-room where several of the other witnesses who had been summoned to give evidence were assembled. She saw Kent, who smiled at her as she came in, and a handsome dark-eyed boy with a sullen expression, whom she knew to be Kent's nephew, who sat reading a Penguin novel and appeared entirely detached from his surroundings. Mrs. Pearce was there, too, her worn face drawn and anxious, wearing the mangy bits of rabbit fur which she wore to church on Sunday evenings and to which she referred, with pathetic pride, as my stole. There was also a youngish man with a Jewish cast of features whom Cherry did not know at all, a large, shabby, elderly man with a grey moustache and a row of medals, and a rabbit-faced girl with peroxided curls. General conversation in this ill-assorted company would have been unlikely under any conditions, but it was made impossible by the presence of a stalwart policeman, looking odd, Cherry thought, without his helmet, who stood by the door.

However, after a while the rabbit-faced girl, who was sitting next to Cherry, edged her chair nearer and began to talk to her in whispers.

"We may have to wait ages. The manager isn't half wild. That's him over there. Mr. Moss. We was told to be here at ten, and now they say the inquest on that poor thing that was killed at the school is to come first. Which are you on, if I may ask?"

"That one, I think," said Cherry, hesitating.

The other stared. "You couldn't be on both."

"I don't really know anything about either case," said Cherry, "but Betty Haydon and I were friends. I very nearly went to the pictures with her—"

"Coo! I'm the one that found her. It was awful—"

The large policeman came over to them. "No talking here, please, miss. Which of you is Miss Garth? You? Will you come this way?"

Kent had left the room some time before and had not come back.

Cherry found herself in a railed-in stand facing a room full of people. A benevolent-looking old gentleman, wearing horn-rimmed spectacles, sat at the end of a table like a chairman at a committee meeting. There were other people who sat and gazed at her and whom she supposed to be the jury, and she learned later that the young men who sat writing busily at a smaller table near the door were representatives of the Press.

"You are a student at the Morosini School, Miss Garth?"

"Yes."

"Last Wednesday afternoon you and your friend, Miss Haydon, were among the last to leave the building?"

"Yes. We were the last. We usually were."

"How was that?"

"We were new. I mean, this is only our second term, so in the dressing-room we have to wait until the others have finished to wash our paint brushes under the tap."

"I see. What happened then?"

"We'd gone a little way when Betty realised that she had left her scarf. She said she'd run back for it because it was a good one and she didn't want it pinched."

"Pinched?"

Cherry's plump cheeks flamed a deeper red. "Stolen, I mean. Several people have missed things lately."

"Very well. You walked on?"

"Yes. I had gone a good way when she caught me up."

The coroner adjusted his spectacles. "Now, listen to me carefully. I want this made clear. It seems possible that Miss Haydon saw or heard something when she went back for her scarf which would throw light on this case, and that if we could have called her we should have learned how Althea Greville came to her end, and who was responsible for her death. Did she pass on this information to you?"

"No. She did not."

"You know nothing at all that would be likely to help the police?"

"Nothing."

The coroner glanced towards the Press table. "Thank you, Miss Garth. That will be all."

She was glad to get away from all the curious eyes. A policeman at the door told her the way out, but she was confused and misunderstood him. As she walked uncertainly down a long passage she met Kent, and he stopped to speak to her.

"It wasn't too bad, I hope," he said kindly, thinking how flurried and forlorn she looked.

"No." She was thinking the same thing about him.

"It's practically over," he explained. "They adjourn indefinitely to give the police a chance to get on with the job. They'll do the same, I expect, with the inquest on Betty Haydon. Her aunt to identify her, some of the cinema staff, and the doctor. Look here"—he said awkwardly—"what about coming over to that tea shop across the Square with me and having something to eat?"

Cherry blushed again, but this time it was with pleasure. "I should like to."

"All right. It's this way, I think."

On their way out they passed a big young man with a red face talking to two policemen who looked after them as they went down the steps, and as they crossed the Square two men with cameras got in their way. Cherry was so unused to publicity that she did not realise what had happened, but she heard Kent mutter "Damn—"

"What is it?"

"Press photographers. Normally, you know, the papers would have been full of this. There hasn't been much actually. Luckily for us the war is more important."

The room over the tea shop was almost empty and they found a table in the window.

"What will you have?"

"Anything. I don't mind."

Cherry pulled off her gloves. She had been miserable, lonely, frightened, and now, unexpectedly, she felt happy. Kent's face, too, looked less drawn. He was smiling. The waitress, languidly waiting for their order, thought them a very ordinary-looking couple. Dull. Kent's hair was growing thin on the top and he was wearing his usual shabby sports coat and flannel slacks, baggy at the knees. He compared very unfavourably with the waitress's boy in the R.A.F.

"Two cold tongue with salad, two rolls and butter. Two white coffees."

"It's nice up here," said Cherry, beaming.

She was not exactly pretty, but she was comfortable. Kent had not known much comfort in his life. It was difficult to imagine her being irritable or impatient, and his half-sister, Agatha, was never anything else. Being with Cherry was like getting into a sheltered corner after facing a biting east wind for a long time. They ate and drank in a leisurely manner, both secretly dreading the moment when they must go back. Cherry to her lodgings, and Kent to Poona to be nagged by Agatha. Arnold would be sulking, too. He had been infuriated by the summons he had received to attend the inquest. It had come at the last moment while they were at breakfast and his mother had urged him to ignore it.

"It's ridiculous. You left the school last year."

He made no reply. Kent had fetched his bicycle from the shed and ridden off without him, but Arnold had followed a few minutes later. In the waiting-room he had read his book and had avoided meeting Kent's eye, and, after all, he had not been called as a witness.

"Mr. Kent—"

Kent was recalled to the present by the timid voice.

"I say—wouldn't you like fruit salad, or something? I'm afraid there isn't much choice here—"

"No more, thanks. I wanted to ask if you really think this will finish the Morosini School?"

"I wouldn't be surprised. It's moribund anyway." He realised, not without surprise, that the kind of life he had been leading for years was coming to an end, and that, so far from minding, he was glad of it. He heard himself saying, "I'm sick of it. I think I shall join the army if they'll have me. Cherry—"

He turned his head as the floor of the tea-room shook under the heavy tread of Sergeant Duffield who had just come up the stairs from the shop.

"Would you come over to the station, sir? There's a question or two you might be able to answer. Sorry to interrupt, miss, but duty's duty, and Griffiths is ready to drive you back."

"Oh," said Cherry blankly, "do I have to have him still?" She was thinking that the man from the Yard had promised her that she would be safe after the inquest. She knew that the questions she had been asked had been framed to show the murderer that he had nothing to fear from her. But—a little cold doubt crept into her own mind—suppose he did not believe her? Suppose he suspected that a trap was being laid for him?

Perhaps the sergeant, who was not as slow as he looked, read her thoughts. He assumed the tone he had used in his uniformed days to old ladies afraid to cross the road.

"It's all right, miss. He won't bother you. He'll keep in the background. We don't want to run any risks, that's all. You go on down now. He's outside with the car."

She held out her hand shyly to Kent, who had been paying the bill.

He gripped it hard, but said nothing.

When she had gone he turned to Duffield and said, "I am ready—"

CHAPTER XV
THE BELL

"It's him all right," said the young railwayman confidently. "It was dark on the platform, see, when I took the passengers' tickets as they passed out, but this chap was helping a woman carry her suitcase. She thanked him and he answered that it was nothing. I had my torch to look at the tickets and I noticed one of them gold signet rings on his finger. He gave me half a cheap day return so I told him the last train back was at nine-twenty—"

"A return from Elder Green?"

"That's right. The eight-fifty-eight was just coming in when he turned up again. He said, 'This saves me a wait,' and I recognised his voice, and I saw the ring again as I clipped his ticket. That's him I saw just now."

Collier brooded over his notes of this conversation as he stood by the window in the superintendent's room waiting for the others to return from the Town Hall after the adjournment of the second inquest. The case was drawing to an end, the solution not far off—or so it seemed, but his mood was not one of exultation.

Pearson came in presently, rubbing his hands.

"Third time lucky—but for us, not for him, eh? I don't mind admitting now that I was getting rattled. My missis wouldn't let the kids out of the house yesterday. Those rumours of a homicidal maniac at large aren't easy to deal with." He glanced at Collier and his tone changed with almost ludicrous abruptness. "I say—is there anything wrong?"

"No, But we must not be too sanguine, Inspector. This identification is not enough in itself—"

"He'll break down if he's properly handled," said Pearson.

The door opened and Sergeant Duffield and Kent came in together.

"Sorry to take up so much of your time, Mr. Kent," said Collier. "Sit down, won't you, and smoke if you want to—"

Kent moved the chair that had been placed for him facing the light.

"Do you mind if I sit round a bit like this? The glare hurts my eyes. I'm quite at your service. I couldn't have worked this afternoon, anyhow. All this is very unsettling."

"Quite!" Collier picked up a ruler from the desk, eyed it thoughtfully as if he wondered what it was, and laid it down again. He was wishing that the local inspector had had duties elsewhere. Pearson had been civil and obliging, but he would have been more than human if he had not been critical of the methods of his colleague from Scotland Yard, and Collier was not so sure of himself as usual.

"How did you spend yesterday evening, Mr. Kent?"

"I went over to Scanminster. I have a friend there, a painter, Gordon Caister. Perhaps you know his stuff. Unfortunately he was out."

"You went directly to his house and then came home again?"

"Not exactly. I called on my way on Miss Haydon—that poor girl's aunt—I thought I ought to express sympathy on behalf of the School. A painful business and I'm so clumsy I should have done it very badly—I'm afraid I was rather relieved that I couldn't make anyone hear. I rang twice."

"About what time, Mr. Kent?"

Kent was either a very good actor or he was genuinely bewildered by this inquisition. "Is it important? I don't quite understand—Good God! Has anything else happened?"

"All right, Mr. Kent. We're coping. Just answer my questions as fully as you can."

"My train got in about seven. It would be a quarter or twenty past, I suppose."

"It was a dark night. You had no difficulty in finding your way?"

"I knew the terrace. I take a sketching class to Scanminster once a week in the summer. I had to use my torch to find the number of the house."

"Did you see or hear anyone about?"

"Not a soul. Scanminster is a sleepy old place at any time. Do you mind telling me—"

"Presently, Mr. Kent. I do the asking here. You went on from there to your friend's house and he wasn't at home. There will be somebody to corroborate that—his wife or his housekeeper?"

"No. He's unmarried and does not keep a servant. I knocked and nobody answered. So then I decided it was not my lucky night, and I went back to the station. A train was just coming in and I got in. It's a two-mile walk from Elder Green station to the village, as you know. I was home about ten and I went straight to bed."

"When you called on Miss Haydon did you go to the front door?"

"Naturally."

"I see. Well, thank you very much, Mr. Kent. You don't feel like adding anything to that statement?"

Kent looked more puzzled than ever. "I don't think I do. You see, I don't know what you want. Must you be so mysterious?"

"I'm sorry," said Collier smoothly, after a brief pause during which he appeared to have made up his mind. "Just for the moment I have not anything to add. I'm much obliged for your co-operation all through this case, Mr. Kent. I won't keep you any longer now. I shall be seeing you again before long." He glanced at Duffield, and the burly sergeant, taking the hint, went out after Kent.

"Plausible," said Pearson admiringly, when the art master had gone. From the window they could see him crossing the Square to the waiting bus, with Duffield following not far behind. "You mean to keep him in view."

"Yes. The trouble is that he may have been telling the truth."

"Easy enough to tell a good circumstantial lie once," said Pearson. "They're apt to slip up when they're asked to repeat it."

Collier nodded. That was true, of course. He had not done with Kent.

"It wouldn't surprise me," said Pearson, who seemed inclined to assume the role of Job's comforter, "it wouldn't surprise me if this wasn't one of those cases where we know who did the job but never get enough evidence to put him in the dock—" he broke off as the telephone on the desk rang, and picked up the receiver. "Yes. Inspector Pearson speaking . . . Yes, he's here . . . It's for you, Mr. Collier."

The call was from the Cottage Hospital at Scanminster. Emma Price seemed a little better. Her pulse was stronger and she showed signs of recovering consciousness. It might be worth his while to come over.

Collier replied that he would come at once. The shabby Ford he had hired from the landlord of the Green Man was waiting for him in the car park outside the Town Hall. Within five minutes he was on his way.

As he went he wondered if the murderer was to find his Nemesis in his latest victim, or if the attack on Emma had, after all, no connection with his case. The identification of Kent had not helped much. If he had denied going to Scanminster in the face of the ticket-collector's evidence they would have been in the straight with the winning post in sight. They could have, been certain then of his guilt. As it was, Collier had to admit to himself that he was still in the dark. He liked Kent, but he was too experienced to assume that as any proof of his innocence. He knew that the mildest and most seemingly harmless of men can be goaded to the point of murder.

The Cottage Hospital was on the outskirts of the town. There were several doctors' cars parked in the drive leading up to the main building. Collier was expected and the young probationer who answered the bell took him straight to the private ward in which Emma Price lay.

The Sister, who had been sitting by the bedside, came to meet him with a rustling of starched print skirts.

"Any time now," she whispered. "Does she know you?"

"Yes. I had a long talk with her the other day."

"She must not be worried or upset—"

"I quite understand." He spoke in a low voice to the constable seated behind the screen. "You are prepared to takes notes? Good. Every word and syllable, whether it seems to make sense or not."

"Yes, sir."

The Sister went out and sent in a nurse, who took up her position on one side of the bed while Collier occupied the chair vacated by the Sister.

Emma's head was heavily bandaged. Lying still on the pillow her face had the rugged austerity of a portrait by Rembrandt. The Flemish master would have rejoiced in that multiplicity of wrinkles. Collier, looking at her, felt his heart harden against her assailant. He was prepared to wait, but she did not keep him long. He had not been in the ward ten minutes when her eyelids quivered and her dry, bloodless lips moved as if trying to form words.

The nurse took one of the work-worn hands lying on the counterpane and felt the pulse.

"All right, dear," she said. "Everything is all right."

Emma made an effort that brought a tinge of colour into her sunken cheeks. "The bell," she muttered. "The bell—"

Collier leaned forward eagerly. The nurse made a warning gesture, but there was no need of it. He knew that Emma had picked up the thread of consciousness where it had broken off.

"The bell. I must go." Her voice changed and grew plangent.

"Don't. I—Help—"

The fluttering of her eyelids and the faint twitchings that had animated her face ceased and she sank back into her coma. The nurse looked across the bed at Collier. "You'd better go now," she said. "She may pass into a natural sleep. In any case you're not likely to get any more at present."

"I shall have to leave a man on duty. Her evidence may be all important."

She nodded. "So long as he stays behind the screen."

He met the Sister in the corridor and asked to see the house surgeon. The doctor did not keep him waiting. He was a brisk young man with a weakness for detective thrillers and an ingenuous respect for the C.I.D. and was much too anxious to hear anything Collier would tell him about the murders of Althea Greville and Betty Haydon to think of standing on his professional dignity.

"You think the attack on this poor old woman ties up with the others?"

"It may do," said Collier cautiously. "But murderers are conservative about their methods. The other two were killed in exactly the same way. Their throats slit by a sharp instrument, possibly a pocket knife, or an old-fashioned razor. I understand that all Emma Price's injuries were caused by her falling or being thrown backwards down the cellar steps?"

"That is so. There are bruises on both forearms just below the elbows consistent with someone having gripped her roughly. Apart from that there's no damage that might not have been caused by an accidental fall."

"But the bruises rule that out?"

"I should say so."

"Will she recover?"

"I can't tell you that. The head injuries are severe. She's on the danger list. If her strength can be maintained she may pull through. But her age is against her. I hope you catch the brute. I wish I could do something to help."

He walked with Collier to his car and shook hands with him warmly.

Collier drove back to Elder Green. He had lunched on a glass of lemonade and a ham sandwich in the interval between the adjournment of the inquest on Betty Haydon and his interview at the police station with Kent, and he felt the need of a more solid meal. He found Duffield waiting for him outside the Green Man and they were soon sitting down together to an ample high tea in their private sitting-room.

The sergeant had travelled back to the village in the same bus with Kent, but in a back seat, and he had trailed him back to Poona. The school was closed on Saturday afternoon.

"I went along to Miss Garth's lodgings then to make sure she'd got back safely, and I had a word with that young Welsh chap they've given her for a watchdog. He told me Kent called on her yesterday afternoon. He wasn't going to let him in, but she said it was all right. Griffiths said he wasn't easy in his mind about it, seeing that you'd given such strict orders nobody was to come near her, and he managed to leave the door of the front parlour open. The kitchen door was open too, and he stood in the passage so that he could hear all they said. He says he got the impression that Mr. Kent was pumping her, trying to find out all he could in an indirect way, and he says the girl talked very freely and remarked that Betty Haydon was more likely to have confided in her aunt's old servant than anyone and that the police might get something from her. Griffiths says Kent got up to go soon after that and seemed to be quite in a hurry all of a sudden."

"The hell he did," said Collier. "On the other hand when Emma recovered consciousness for a minute, she said something about a bell that seemed to me to be in his favour. You remember he told us he rang twice and could get no answer. It's possible, you know, that if that is true he saved Emma's life. Her assailant, hearing the bell, may have been alarmed and have made off without waiting to finish her off in the usual manner."

"We've only his word for it that he rang," said Duffield. He had expected Collier to attach more importance to Kent's conversation with Cherry Garth and he looked slightly deflated. They had worked so often together that Collier knew all his reactions.

"You think he heard the bell ring at the moment he was attacking her and claims that he rang it? A form of alibi. But would he dare? He would know that the person who really rang would come forward eventually. I wonder if the front door bell can be heard in the houses on either side. You might go over to-morrow morning, Duffield, and find out. But we must not concentrate too exclusively on Kent." He pushed back his chair and filled his pipe. "Are you really convinced of his guilt?"

"I wouldn't say convinced, but there's more against him than any of the others," said the sergeant obstinately.

"What grounds have you for saying that?"

"He could have killed the model. He says he went home, but he hasn't any witnesses to prove it. Mrs. Mansfield and the young fellow were out until some hours later, and they don't keep a servant. He could cut across the fields from the school to the lane. There's gaps in the hedges and the land is rough pasture that doesn't show footprints. According to his own admission he was in Scanbridge at the Pictures the evening Betty Haydon was murdered. He says he went to the other cinema, but we haven't found anyone who saw him there. Last night he was in Scanminster at the time of the attack on the maid at number 17. As to motive, he may have known Althea Greville better than he makes out. Say they were lovers and he'd grown tired of her. Or maybe he was still sweet on her, and she'd got tired of him. He comes back to the life classroom after the students are gone, Althea tells him off—and a woman like her knows just how to flick a man on the raw—he sees red, and the rest follows. And then, as he comes out into the passage he gets a glimpse of one of the students who has come back for her scarf. After a bit he realises that she must be silenced."

"That's a weak spot in your case," said Collier, meta-phorically putting his finger on it. "And yet, I don't know. It might have been a mere glimpse, as you say. She was an ordinary-looking girl. Nine young women out of ten wear brown coats and berets. But he may have recognised her when he saw her again the following day. In that case I don't envy his feelings during the time that elapsed between that recognition and the moment when he ran his quarry to ground in the balcony of the Corona. She had only to go to the nearest policeman, Pearson, or the constable on duty at the gate, or you or me when we turned up, and say, 'When I went back to the school on Wednesday afternoon I saw Mr. Kent coming out of the life classroom.' He must have expected her to do it. God knows why she didn't. The power complex, I suppose. Feeling she held his life in her hands. She got a kick out of that, I daresay."

"You've got to admit that it looks bad that the old servant got hers so soon after Miss Garth said that to Kent about her being the most likely one to have heard what the girl had seen," argued Duffield. "Cause and effect follow-ing pretty close."

"Yes, if the attack upon her is a part of our case. But we aren't certain of that. I distrust coincidences, but they do occur. All you have proved, Duffield, is that Kent could have done it. That wouldn't be enough for the Public Pros-ecutor, as you know very well. I could build up as good a case against Kent's nephew, Arnold Mansfield. He was running about with Althea when she was here last summer. He isn't at the school now but he's staying at home. He knows his way about the school buildings and is as able to slip in and out after dark as his uncle. He has no alibi for the two murders, and he was out yesterday evening while I was at Poona talking to his mother. He might have cycled to Scanminster and back. His mother has spoiled him and he's naturally bad-tempered. He could be vindictive. Notice his mouth next time you meet him."

Duffield rubbed his nose and sighed.

"Morosini is still on my list," said Collier. "No alibi for the first murder and an obviously phoney one for about the time when somebody must have taken the seat behind Betty Haydon in the back row of the balcony of the Corona. But it is in his favour that he could hardly have known she would be there unless she rang him up and arranged to meet him, in which case she would have been to some extent on her guard. If she had turned to face him there would have been time to scream. Would she have had the nerve to play such a big fish as the great Morosini himself? It is possible. But those Italian servants of his will swear black is white if he tells them to. The question is can we get any farther with any of these people?"

"Would Morosini know about Betty Haydon being likely to confide in her aunt's maid?"

"No. That is a point. Unless he talked to Betty or rather led her on to talk. They might have met somewhere outside the cinema, you know, if it was by appointment. It was a cold night with a drizzle of rain. He might have suggested taking shelter and finishing their talk where they wouldn't be overheard or disturbed. The poor little fool would be thrilled by her own daring, fascinated, overawed by genius at close quarters. Morosini is a remote and god-like being to the average student at his school. If she did challenge him it was with the sparrow-like cheekiness of a schoolboy trying to get a king's autograph. But all this is supposition and no real use. Well, to-morrow is another day, and meanwhile I have to write my report for the Super. You might go down to the bar, Sergeant. You might pick up something more about young Mansfield."

CHAPTER XVI
THE NEST IN THE HEDGEROW

COLLIER and the sergeant were sitting over a late breakfast when the landlord put his head in at the door.

"It's that Eyetalian chap from Mr. Morosini's place," he announced. "He's asking for you, Inspector. Seems upset like."

"Send him up by all means."

The sergeant's gloom lightened perceptibly. "He's been a bit offish up to now, hasn't he? It might be a break at that."

Duffield went regularly to the pictures with his wife on his evenings off duty, and was gradually acquiring a transatlantic vocabulary.

Collier looked forward hopefully to the time when his sergeant would refer to his colleagues as bulls.

Beppi came in quickly and stood with his back to the door and one slim brown hand gripping the handle.

"Will you come with me now, quickly? Something has happened to my master. I am afraid—"

Both men rose at once, and he led the way downstairs and into the village street. There was nobody about. The children were in Sunday school, their fathers on their allotments, their mothers preparing the hot Sunday dinner. It was not raining, but a clammy grey mist made for poor visibility.

"What is wrong exactly?" asked Collier.

"I do not know. I heard the padrone answering the telephone an hour ago, and then he ran downstairs and shut himself in the studio. I heard noises as if—as if something was going on, a struggle perhaps, and the voice of the padrone crying out as if he were angry or in pain. When I tried the door it was locked. I went round to the other door opening into the garden, but the inside shutters were closed. I called to him, begging him to let me in, but there was no answer. I did not know what to do. I thought then if I fetched you that you would break down the door—"

They were hurrying up the avenue from the great wrought iron gates. The formal Italian garden and the ornate facade of Bello Sguardo looked oddly artificial under the leaden November sky, with the falsity of exhibition buildings in the unkind light of day. Collier turned up his coat collar. It was an unconscious reaction to the shivering nudity of the statues on their pedestals among the dripping laurels.

"Are you alone here with Mr. Morosini?"

"Si, signore."

"You must have plenty to do."

"He is often in London. Then I clean the house. When he is here I cook the meals, clean the car, wait on him. I can do everything," said Beppi with pride. "This way—"

Duffield stared about him as they crossed the hall with its mosaic floor, twisted Byzantine pillars, and gilded lanthorns. He had been unprepared for such magnificence. Beppi led them to the studio door. He knocked on it, his swarthy face drawn with anxiety.

"Padrone—"

There was no answer.

Collier looked grave. "You should have rung us up," he said. "It would have been quicker."

"I did not think. I lost my head."

Collier nodded to his sergeant, who produced a bit of twisted wire from his pocket and bent to the lock. It yielded to treatment after a little manipulation and the door swung slowly open.

"Madonna mia!" groaned the manservant. The two C.I.D. men said nothing. The studio reminded them both of a gambling den they had had to search for a hidden store of cocaine after a fight between rival gangs followed by a police raid. Chairs overturned, cushions scattered over the floor and trampled underfoot, easels thrown down and one large canvas slit to ribbons, and a large blue and gold Chinese jar shattered. The curtains were all drawn over the windows and the big skylight and all the lights were switched on. Morosini was sitting on the edge of the wooden platform that served as a model's throne, with his face buried in his hands, a forlorn and gaudy figure in red silk pyjamas and a red velvet dressing-gown. A wicked-looking two-edged knife with an ornate silver gilt handle lay beside him on the dais.

Collier went up to him and picked up the weapon gingerly, using his handkerchief. The shining steel blade was clean.

"What's all this, Mr. Morosini?"

The sergeant glanced at him in surprise, for he had spoken with an unexpected gentleness, as if to a child.

The painter lifted a ravaged face and they saw that he had been crying. "I—I was going to kill myself," he said huskily.

Beppi uttered a loud cry of distress. "Padrone, padrone—"

Collier quelled him with a look. "Don't stand there bellowing like a calf. Go into the kitchen and make some coffee and bring your master a cup. Something to eat, too. Go with him, Duffield."

He sat down on the platform beside Morosini and proceeded to fill his pipe. He thought he knew what he had to deal with now. His quick eyes had noted that the devastation that surrounded them was more apparent than real. "A brain storm," he thought, "but if he is subject to them, and Althea got in his way—"

He said, "Wouldn't that be rather hard on your friends? What about Lady Violet?"

Morosini covered his face again and said indistinctly, "She is the cause. You English. So cold, so cruel. I cannot live without her."

His grief and agitation were genuine enough, and though his lack of self-control seemed almost indecent to Collier he felt sorry enough for him to make a real attempt to stiffen his morale. "It may not be as bad as you think. She rang you up, I suppose?"

"Yes. How did you know?"

"Your servant told us you came down here and shut yourself in after answering the telephone. You nearly frightened him out of his wits, poor devil."

Morosini blew his nose. "He is my fratello di latte— what you call foster brother."

"I prescribe a cigarette," said Collier cheerfully. "Will you have one of my fags?"

"No, thank you. I only smoke Turkish. In a box on the table over there—"

Collier was amused by the painter's cool assumption that he was to be waited on, but it gave him the opportunity he wanted to see if Morosini had written a farewell message or letter. There was nothing of the kind on the table and the pen on the pen tray was dry. He remembered his earlier impression that Morosini was a confirmed poseur, and wondered if he had ever really meant to commit suicide. He brought back the box of cigarettes and struck a match.

Morosini seemed a little calmer. He inhaled deeply. "You appear to be human," he remarked.

Collier grinned. "I hope so. She broke off the engagement, I suppose. Did she give any reason?"

It was fortunate he thought, that Morosini did not seem inclined to blame the activities of the police for his troubles. Luckily he had made the right approach, and was regarded as a sufficiently sympathetic audience.

"She will not believe that my car broke down the other evening. 'Don't try and put that one over with me, Aldo,' she said, 'I've been out with you umpteen times. You're pretty good with a car. Or, if you did have a real breakdown you'd leave your bus by the roadside and wangle a lift,' she said. I assured her—but poum, she rang off. Finished, she said. Finished. I tell you I must have her. I have never loved, really loved, before—"

"Well, you can hardly blame her," said Collier reasonably, "if she thinks you put in the time stabbing another girl in the balcony of a cinema."

The ice was thin here, would it bear him? He held his breath. Morosini, mercifully, did not choose this moment for a display of righteous indignation.

"Diamine. But it is incredible that she should think such a thing of me. Am I a Neapolitan cabman to go about knifing people? I am Morosini. My work is important. It is of the first importance."

"Of course," said Collier soothingly, "but that story of the car breakdown was pretty thin, you know. I didn't believe it myself."

"No? Well, I will tell you the truth. You are a man, you will understand—"

At this point Collier's conscience gave him a reminder which he dared not ignore. "Just a moment," he said firmly. "I'm most interested, but I must warn you that anything you say to me may be used against you if a charge is preferred—"

But Morosini was beginning to enjoy himself. "Macche," he made light of the warning. "It is not what perhaps you have thought. I could see you suspected me—" he broke off as Beppi came in wheeling a service trolley. "Coffee, butter, rolls, honey. Excellent. Beppi, bring cups for these gentlemen, or perhaps only for the inspector. You will attend to the needs of his colleague—" Collier intervened. "That's very kind, Mr. Morosini, but we've had breakfast. If you will allow him, the sergeant will help your man clear up the mess here while we continue our conversation."

Morosini waved his hand. "Certainly, certainly."

Duffield, taking the hint, pottered about the studio, picking up torn and trampled cushions and setting chairs on their legs again. There was an odd expression on his large face and his lips moved without sound. "Of all the loony bins—"

Beppi, meanwhile, after pouring out his master's coffee, had gone back to his kitchen.

Collier pulled at his pipe. He was hoping that the interruption had not checked the flow of confidences. For a man who half an hour previously had been thinking of taking his own life, Morosini had a remarkably good appetite.

"I usually breakfast earlier than this," he explained, with his mouth full.

Collier had risen to pick up a frame from which the slit canvas hung in tattered shreds. "You made a thorough job of this," he said.

The painter shrugged his shoulders. "I lost my temper. Another portrait I had begun of Violet. Luckily it was only half finished."

Collier eyed him thoughtfully. There was something child-like and attractive about the fellow in his present mood of good-humoured candour, but the hand that was now engaged in spreading honey on a piece of toast must have plunged the knife savagely again and again into a woman's breast. Only a picture, of course, only canvas smeared with paint. Still, it was, perhaps, symptomatic. He sat down again. "You were going to tell me what actually happened on Friday night," he said casually. "You left the Ritz soon after four and did not arrive here until past eleven—"

"I will tell you. I have a little friend of some years' standing. She runs a hairdresser's shop, one of a new block in a new suburb. She lives in the flat over the shop, and I pay the rent of both. It is on the main road and I pass it when I drive to and fro to Town. You understand, it is convenient. Friday night was cold and wet. Lady Violet is adorable, but, naturally, I treat her with the utmost respect. My wife to be. On my way here I called on my little friend. Why not? But when you questioned me I realised that Violet would be angry. An Italian girl—they know that a man cannot be monogamous—but the English are intolerant. So I invented the breakdown and the long wait and the lorry driver. I wanted to avoid trouble."

"I see," said Collier, in a slightly more official tone. He felt tolerably certain that he was getting the truth at last. "But it's always a mistake, sir, to lie to the police, and in a case like this it may have serious results. If we could have eliminated you at the start it would have saved valuable time."

"But only a moron," said Morosini blandly, "forgive me, my dear Inspector, I must say it—only a moron could imagine that I would go about murdering the models and the students of my own school. It is so obviously the wrong kind of publicity."

Collier laughed in spite of himself.

Morosini lit another cigarette and stretched luxuriously. "This need not go any further?" he suggested. "You would earn my gratitude—"

His tone was so significant that Collier froze instantly.

"I can't promise anything," he said stiffly. "Your story needs corroboration. I shall have to have the address of this hair-dressing establishment."

Morosini was unabashed. "I'll take you along and introduce you to Nina, if you like. She's Italian by birth but a British subject by marriage. She was a widow when I met her. Her husband was an English jockey in the service of the Marchese Gualtieri."

Collier thought a minute. "Very well," he said, "if we can go now."

"Right. I'll go up and dress."

"I must ask you not to telephone."

Morosini smiled. "There is no need. On a Sunday morning she is not likely to be out, and I do not have to prepare her for our arrival. She has only to tell the truth."

"Oh, quite."

But when Morosini had gone up to his room Collier went out to the hall, beckoning to Duffield to follow him. "We can hear the phone anywhere in the house from here, I fancy," he said. "The main instrument is in that sedan chair, and the others are extensions. I shall leave you here with Beppi. See to it that he does not use the telephone either. I think this clears Morosini, but I'll hear what the girl friend has to say first."

"I wouldn't be too sure," said Duffield doubtfully. "He's got what I'd call a nasty temper. Handy with a knife, too."

"I agree. But he couldn't be in two places at once. All right. Carry on."

Morosini came gaily down the stairs. In his belted overcoat he looked rather like an actor, Collier thought.

"If you'll come round to the garage with me we can get off at once."

Collier quite enjoyed his drive. The painter's car was a de luxe model of a famous make, supplied with all the latest gadgets.

"You are an owner-driver perhaps?" he said as his passenger settled down beside him.

"I run a baby Austin of ancient vintage to take my wife into the country when I get a week-end off."

"You are married? I was thinking of it as you know, but perhaps for an artist—"

He sighed and was silent for a few minutes, but he soon recovered and talked all the rest of the way. He had only one subject and that was Aldo Morosini. Collier listened with amused interest. He wondered how two such complete egoists as the painter and Lady Violet could ever have imagined that they were made for one another. What Morosini needed was a self-effacing and mouse-like little woman who was willing to spend her life with him in a state of perpetual admiration. He presently discovered that this was an accurate description of Nina.

Morosini's secret orchard was unromantic in appearance, a flat over a shop in a gaunt new block of commercial buildings, a part of the deplorable ribbon development along the main road twenty miles nearer London than Elder Green. Nina, who did not keep a maid, opened the door to them herself. Her plain, sallow little face was irradiated at the sight of Morosini, who greeted her with a careless kiss and introduced his companion as "my friend, Mr. Collier."

The glamorous young woman who had been his official betrothed would hardly have suspected a rival in this subfusc female and even Collier with his considerable experience of the oddity of human nature, was surprised.

"You can give us lunch, cara?"

"Of course. In half an hour. Soup, omelet, salad and zabaione. Will that do?"

"Delicious. She's a marvellous cook," Morosini explained in parenthesis. "By the way, Nina, did I leave my driving gloves here on Friday evening. It was Friday, wasn't it?"

"Yes. But you didn't leave any gloves," she said anxiously.

"How long was I here, cara? I have a reason for asking."

"We were just closing so it must have been about half-past five. I found you here, you remember, when I came up. I had been doing a perm and I was tired, but we had a lovely evening here by the fire—" she gazed up at him adoringly and he patted her arm. Neither of them paid the slightest attention to Collier, standing by.

"You wanted me to stay but I left after hearing the last act of *Rigoletto* broadcast by the B.B.C. When was that?"

"At eleven. I must go, or the lunch will be late."

He turned to Collier when she had left them to prepare the meal. "Are you satisfied?"

"Thank you, sir. That seems good enough," said Collier. He was thinking that he could check up on the time of Morosini's arrival, if necessary. Nina's assistants were sure to keep their eyes open for the comings and goings of their employer's boy friend with the posh car. "I've got what I wanted and I ought to be going," he added. "You don't really want me to stay to lunch?"

"I most certainly do. You must really taste her zabaione. It melts in the mouth. A miracle of golden sweetness."

Morosini seemed pleased with himself and the world in general. He was looking at his reflection in the glass over the mantelpiece while he ran a pocket comb through the crisp black waves of hair with their becoming touch of silver over the ears.

"Afterwards, if you don't mind," he said, "you might find your own way back if you are returning to Elder Green. A bus passes the door every hour. I think I may go on to Town," he broke off as Nina bustled in, flushed with her exertions, and laden with a tray. There was an agreeable sound of frying in the tiny kitchen and the flat was pervaded by a most savoury smell. He continued, slightly lowering his voice, when she had gone back to her cooking stove, "I have been thinking it over and I do not regard what was said this morning as final. La donna é mobile. If I call on a certain fair lady I may find her in a more yielding mood. If I refer her to you I know you will be able to assure her that I have not murdered anybody, and as to this—ah—nest in the hedgerow, I rely on your discretion."

"What did you tell the blighter?" enquired the indignant sergeant later, when he and his superior officer were sitting over their tea in their parlour at the Green Man. Collier had duly returned to the village by bus and had fetched his colleague from Bello Sguardo on his way back to the inn.

"Nothing. There's nothing illegal in his amatory activities. And my time was not wasted. I think we can write him off our list, and the lunch came up to my highest expectations. That little woman is worth a hundred dizzy blondes. If he marries his Lady Violet they'll give each other hell, so justice will be done one way if not in another."

Duffield grunted, and helped himself liberally to jam. "All very well, but we aren't here to clear people. What is the next move, sir? There's still Kent and his nephew, and the school caretaker."

"Yes. I think we might devote some attention to the man Pearce to-morrow. He gives an impression of mental instability and his wife's evidence is valueless. She'd say anything to keep him out of the soup."

He had left the tea-table and sat by the fire turning over the pages of his notebook, a worried frown on his lean face. There was still no real evidence against anyone. He had to admit to himself that he hardly knew what to do next. Emma, if she recovered from her injuries, might be able to help them, but he doubted it. She had been carrying a candle, but it was dark in the alley, and it was unlikely that she had seen her assailant's face.

As he pondered his notes on the case he had a worrying feeling that he had missed something, that he had picked up the false clues and left the one that really mattered trailing. Was there anything to be gained by turning back? In all these statements taken from the students at the school, the staff of the cinema, was there one revealing sentence, one operative word that had been passed over, unnoticed, at the time?

CHAPTER XVII
THE POINTING ANGEL

THAT Monday, during which, if he had but known it, his case was to reach a climax, opened unhopefully for Collier. He received a report from the Yard on the painting aprons and overalls that had been collected from the school dressing-rooms and sent up for examination. The experts had failed to find any trace of bloodstains, nor were there any traces of human blood in the matter scraped out of the waste pipes of the wash-basins. According to the medical evidence it was unlikely that the murderer had got away with clean hands, and the fact that he apparently had been in no hurry to wash them, evinced an unusual degree of callousness.

Collier was still frowning over this negative report and its implications when he was rung up by the friendly superintendent from Scanminster, who wanted to tell him that Emma Price's nephew had been interviewed at his Pimlico lodgings. He had a job as a waiter at a West End hotel, and he had been able to prove that he was on duty on Friday evening and could not possibly have been in or near Scanminster at the time of the attack on his aunt. The police were still looking for the hawker who had threatened her. They had had complaints about him from several householders. The Hospital authorities did not think much of Emma Price's chance of recovery. She was definitely, weaker and had had no further intervals of consciousness.

Sergeant Duffield, looking out of their sitting-room window, saw the Morosini students who lodged in the village, drifting along the road in twos and threes. The church clock was striking nine. "I suppose the school is open as usual?"

"What's that?" said Collier absently. "Yes. No point in closing down. Kent asked me and I told him he could carry on."

"The landlord was telling me that Althea Greville is to be buried in the churchyard here some time this afternoon. The vicar's taking the service. It's like the army, they always assume you're C. of E. if there's no evidence to the contrary. I don't suppose she was much of a church or chapel goer, poor thing. They've given out that it's to be to-morrow. The parson's afraid they might get crowds of sightseers trampling over the graves."

Collier was not listening. He said, "You spent a good part of yesterday with that fellow Beppi. There's no doubt, I suppose, that he's devoted to his master? Morosini told us they were foster-brothers. That's a very real tie, I believe, in some countries."

"He's devoted all right. He spent most of the time that you were away with his master telling me how wonderful he was. I've no use for his nibs myself, but I suppose the blighter can paint."

"Yes. We must allow him that. The question is, would he be devoted enough to commit a crime for him?"

Duffield whistled. "I never thought of that. It could be. Beppi's alone there. The gardener is English and lives down the village. Beppi's got a bicycle and he goes to the pictures. We got talking about them. And he's lived here long enough to know his way about."

"Did you part on friendly terms?"

"Oh, quite."

"You might look him up again. He'll have time on his hands if Morosini stayed up in Town last night. Find out if he went to any cinema in Scanbridge last week. Talk about the murders and see what reactions you get. But I don't want him to think he is suspected."

"Very good, sir. I'll do that."

Collier was not really very hopeful of results in that direction, but it was worth trying. He went off himself to call on the Mansfields, and this time he found Arnold at home. Mrs. Mansfield was upstairs with the daily woman, making the beds. Collier heard him shouting that there was somebody at the door and his mother telling him to go.

"And if it's the grocer tell him he must wait. I'll pay next week—"

Arnold was wearing bedroom slippers and a silk scarf instead of a collar, and he needed a shave. He gave Collier an unwelcoming look and called back over his shoulder, "It's the cop again."

Collier smiled. Crude bad manners always put him on his mettle. "I'll come in if you don't mind."

"My uncle isn't here. He's gone down to the school," said Arnold sulkily, but he stepped back reluctantly and allowed Collier to squeeze past him and walk into the room on the left where the Mansfields and their friends had been playing bridge once when he called before. It had not been dusted recently and Collier noticed ash trays overflowing with cigarette ends and sticky circles on the piano where cocktail glasses had been set down. A large photograph of Mrs. Mansfield in her younger days, with bare shoulders rising from clouds of chiffon, stood on a side table among a jumble of silver knick-knacks.

Arnold did not ask his visitor to sit down.

"Mother told me you came Friday evening and asked for me. What the hell is it all about? It's getting past a joke," he said fretfully.

"I'm sorry it annoys you," said Collier in his mildest voice. "I find people are generally quite willing to help the police in a case of this sort."

"I don't know anything."

"There may be some apparently trifling matter, something that seems quite unimportant to you that would give us a pointer. You must not think you are our only victim, Mr. Mansfield," said Collier, with his most disarming smile. "We have to worry a lot of people like this."

"Oh, well," said Arnold ungraciously, "ask away, and get it over."

"You were a student at the school when Miss Greville was posing for the life class last summer?"

"Yes, I was. What of it?"

"She lodged with the caretaker and his wife?"

"I believe so. Yes."

"Did she ever say anything that suggested that Pearce had—shall we say fallen for her?"

Arnold thought a moment. "I believe she did. She laughed about it and said it wasn't her fault, she hadn't encouraged him, and she hoped old mother Pearce wouldn't put poison in her tea."

"That's very interesting. But I daresay several of the students fancied themselves in love with her."

"Well—she was darned attractive. Somehow you couldn't help watching her, the way she moved. She was amusing, too. She'd seen a lot of life. She was at a loose end in the evenings and sometimes we made up parties and took her to road-houses to swim and dance."

"Every evening?"

"Oh, Lord, no. We couldn't have afforded it. She expected the best of everything, and those places rook you. Even sharing exes it strained our resources."

Collier's careful handling was having its effect. Young Mansfield was speaking more naturally and less aggressively.

"Did any of the girl students come too?"

"No. They're fairly broad-minded, but Althea was a bit too much for them, I fancy," grinned Arnold. "Anyway, they weren't asked. She wasn't the sort to want other women around."

"One of the students had a car, I suppose," said Collier casually.

"If you could call it a car. Lynton Cope picked it up for twelve pounds. It covered the ground. A four-seater, but we could squeeze in three at the back."

"Lynton Cope isn't at the school now."

"No. He went to America. He had an uncle over there. Channing and Roe joined the R.A.F. Channing crashed a few weeks ago. I saw it in the paper. I don't know what became of Hunter."

"The four of you young fellows clubbed together to take the model out and have a little fun. Looking back now, would you say that any one of your party fell seriously in love with her?"

Arnold took another cigarette from his case and lit it. Collier noticed that his hands were not as steady as they might have been.

"I don't know," he said at last. "I daresay more than one of us thought he was. We didn't mean anything to her. Just something to pass the time and pay for her drinks."

"Did you know that she was working here again last week?"

Arnold swallowed hard and hesitated. It was obvious to Collier that he was wondering if it would be better to tell a lie. Finally he said, with a return to his earlier boorishness, "I didn't know beforehand or I should have kept out of her way. I'd had enough. I met her down the village Tuesday morning after morning school. I was surprised. I'd no idea Uncle John would be such a mutt as to engage her again, but I gather she wrote and told him a hard luck story. She stopped and spoke to me and I had to be just civil. She looked older and not nearly so smart, and she tried to touch me for ten shillings. Luckily I was able to tell her that I hadn't a bean."

"And that was the last time you saw her alive?"

"It was."

"I suppose that though you are no longer a student you are often in and out of the school?"

"Wrong again," said Arnold. "The arty crowd aren't in my line. I prefer the theatre and film people. And I see quite enough of Uncle John at home without seeking him out at the place where he works, thank you."

"I see. When were you last in the school buildings?"

"Ages ago." Arnold's voice was no longer quite under control. His eyes were restless, seeming to seek some means of escape. "In September, soon after term began, I was home for a few days. I went over one day with a message from my mother. We were going out to dinner. I saw my uncle in his room, but I didn't stay."

"Did you go round by the village or take the short cut from here across the fields?"

"I don't remember."

"Did you go into the school last Wednesday with a message, or for any other reason?"

"Certainly not. If anybody says I did he's a liar." Arnold's half-smoked cigarette broke in half between his fingers. He looked at it and flung it into the fender.

"I see," said Collier gently. He did not feel that he could go any farther without warning his victim that any admissions he made could be used against him in evidence, and he did not want to do that just yet. "I won't bother you any more just now," he said. "By the way, I have to go over to Scanminster and I may use a push bike. Is there a shorter way than the road past Elder Green station and over the level crossing past the mill?"

"You can go round by Bantling's Corner. It may be a bit shorter, but it's a secondary road with a rotten surface. I thought you chaps from the Yard swanked about in high-powered cars."

"We all have to watch the petrol gauge these days," said Collier smiling. "Good-bye for the present."

He walked slowly up the lane. Young Mansfield had given him food for thought. The readiness with which he had answered his final question suggested that his conscience was clear in regard to the attack on Emma Price, but before that his increasing uneasiness had been so evident that Collier was beginning to wonder if he would have to look any further for his man. But there was still not an atom of the material proof that is needed to convince a jury. The Scanbridge people had been thorough over the fingerprints, and had compared all those they had found in the life classroom and the two dressing-rooms with those they had taken of the students, Pearce and his wife, and the two masters, and, of course, those of the murdered woman herself. There had been no extraneous prints.

Arnold had admitted meeting Althea in the village the day before her death. According to him she had tried to borrow ten shillings from him without success. Wasn't it equally possible that they had arranged a meeting in the school the following afternoon after the students had left? The drawback to that theory was that the caretaker normally made his rounds and locked up about five o'clock. Arnold might, however, have learned from his uncle that Pearce was having one of his bouts of malaria, or whatever it was that laid him low at intervals. One had to be careful with young Mansfield, Collier reflected, his manners were against him, and it would be easy to misjudge him, but obviously there was a case for further investigation.

He went back to the inn and was given a telephone message that had come a few minutes earlier. It was from the superintendent at Scanminster. Emma Price was sinking and was not likely to last out the day. The doctors thought she might recover consciousness before the end. It was just a chance if he thought it worth while to come over.

Collier hesitated. The policeman on duty in the ward could take down anything she said, but he would not know what questions to ask. He decided to go. The Green Man's car was at his disposal. He left a message for Duffield, and set off.

The house surgeon saw him before he was taken up to the ward. "You may have some time to wait," he said, "and she may pass out without uttering another word."

"Can I rely on what she says if she does speak? Her brain—"

"The head injuries are superficial. Her spine was damaged. She's dying from shock more than anything. She called herself fifty-nine, but we think she was a good deal older than that. Anyway, I know no reason why she shouldn't talk sense if she talks at all."

"Thank you."

Emma Price did not seem to have moved since he last saw her. He nodded to the policeman sitting patiently behind the screen with his notebook open on his knees before he sat down by the bedside to wait. The quiet room, bare as a convent cell, was conducive to thought. Five days had gone by since the first murder was committed. Since then another woman had died, and a third was dying. Only one thing was certain, and that was that the killer was somewhere close at hand. Most probably he was one of the people he had interviewed. Someone who knew his way about the school, who had been able to follow Betty Haydon into the Corona, who had learned somehow that she talked freely to her aunt's old servant. Who could have known that? The answer, of course, was Kent.

And yet he was unconvinced.

There has been cases when, with little evidence, he had been sure. This was not one of them. His list of suspects had been reduced to four. That was as near as he had got to solving the mystery even in his own mind.

The bed creaked as the woman lying on it moved. The nurse who had been standing by lifted a warning hand. "It may be now—" she whispered.

Emma Price's eyes opened wide. The wrinkled face was smiling. Then, very gradually, the light faded from it as the glow of colour fades from a landscape when a cloud covers the sun.

The nurse felt for the pulse in the lean wrist and shook her head.

Emma had gone, and if she knew who had struck her down she took that knowledge with her.

"She saw something at the end," said Collier. "Something—pleasant."

The nurse said, "Yes. They often do. You'd better go now. I have to fetch Sister."

When he had left the Cottage Hospital Collier looked at his watch and was surprised to find that it was past three. He had missed his lunch and he decided to get a cup of tea and something to eat at a confectioner's shop in the High Street.

He was back in Elder Green about four o'clock. He left the car in the yard of the Green Man. He had decided that it was time he had another talk with Cherry Garth, and he wanted a word with P.C. Griffiths. He thought he would take a short cut across the fields to her lodgings. The landlord had told him that he would save a quarter of a mile by crossing the churchyard.

The sexton had just finished filling in a new grave a little apart from the others on the north side of the church. Collier paused to speak to him.

"Was there a crowd?"

"There warn't nobody. Parson diddled 'em, see. He gave it out 'twould be to-morrow, and he fixed it with the police at Scanbridge to bring her over this morning early. 'Twas all finished by eight o'clock, same as it will be some day, I reckon, for the chap as did her in. Not but what she asked for trouble, and if them as asks for it gets it, they can't complain."

"You knew about her?"

The sexton shifted his grip on the handle of his spade. "Ar. There was a lot of talk when she was here before."

The grass where they were standing was long and wet. Collier moved back on to the stone threshold of a narrow door, sheltered from the east by a flying buttress.

"If you want to go into the church you'll have to walk round," said the sexton. "That's the devil's door and it's kept locked."

Most of the graves on the unpopular north side were humble mounds covered with ivy or neglected grass. On two or three there were dirty jam pots holding the skeletal remains of long dead flowers. There was one exception, a brand-new white marble angel pointing heavenwards, in a neat railed-in space covered with white marble chips. The discordant effect of this monument of bad taste was slightly mitigated by a large bunch of wine-coloured button chrysanthemums laid at the foot of the pedestal.

"That's impressive in its way," said Collier.

"Ar," said the grave-digger curtly, "cost a tidy bit, I reckon. Where was you going, if I may ask?"

"I was told there was a short cut across the churchyard and the fields beyond to the station."

"Ar. But two of them fields have been ploughed up. You'll find it rough going, and you can't pick your way with darkness coming on."

"Thanks. You're probably right. I'll go by road."

The sexton shouldered his coat and his spade and trudged away.

Collier decided to go back to the inn and drive down to the station cottages, but something in the sexton's manner had awakened his interest in the marble monstrosity and he turned aside from the path to look at it more closely.

The name on it was familiar to him, but that was not surprising. In Elder Green, as in most villages, three or four surnames occurred over and over again. Under the text *He is Risen*, cut into the stone, there was an almost illegible scribble in blue indelible pencil. Collier copied it into his notebook before he passed on.

He found Duffield in the inn yard.

"They gave you my message?"

"Yes. I didn't think you'd be back so soon."

Collier explained why he had changed his mind about walking down to Cherry Garth's lodgings. "We'll go now. You'd better come with me. You've nothing to report, I suppose?"

"Nothing."

"Emma Price died this afternoon, while I was there," said Collier gloomily. "This is a hell of a case." He switched on the dimmed headlights and let in the clutch. "By the way, Duffield, remind me to look up Ezekiel xvi. 41, 42, 43."

Chapter XVIII
CHERRY GOES BACK

ALL the students turned up on Monday. The life class-room, in which the murder had been committed, was still closed, but apart from that there was nothing to show that anything had happened to disturb the normal routine. Another model had been engaged for the life class, and old Stryver was still sitting for the less advanced students in the Prelim. Cherry Garth had pinned a fresh piece of canvas on her drawing-board and was trying to paint his head from a different angle. She was dreading the break, she thought she would miss Betty so much, for they had always sat together to eat their elevenses, but one of the older girls came up to her and asked her to join her and her friends, and one of the men looked at her work and gave her some advice about the blocking in, and they all tried to be kind, so it was not so bad after all.

Kent came in once, but he looked busy and harassed, and he paid her no special attention. Her spirits sank again after that. She told herself that she had no reason to suppose that he was really interested in her. He had asked her to lunch with him on Saturday after the inquest, but there was nothing in that, nothing at all.

She tried to keep her mind on her work, but old Stryver was not a very inspiring model, he was reputed to be eccentric and he was certainly very grimy and neglected-looking, with a week's growth of beard on his long upper lip and jutting predacious jaw and coarse grey hair straggling over the collar of his ancient black broad-cloth coat. There was no need for him to look like that, for according to Cherry's landlady, who was his niece by marriage, the old man had money in the bank, besides what he earned by doing odd jobs, and he could have lived with his married daughter, Mrs. Meggott, if he had not preferred to retain his independence and manage for himself in a picturesque but insanitary cottage on the outskirts of the village.

It was not very easy to find models in the neighbour-hood, and the women and girls were unreliable and apt to come for two or three days and not again. Old Stryver had his faults. He was apt to glare and mutter when he was told that he was not keeping the pose. But he never let the class down by failing to come and for some time past he had been regarded as an invaluable stop-gap in an emergency. When he was working at the school he expected to be left in undisputed possession of the preliminary classroom during the lunch hour to champ with toothless jaws at the bread and cheese he brought with him, tied up in a dingy red bandanna handkerchief, and Cherry took her parcel of sandwiches over to Mrs. Meggott's cottage and ate them sitting by the fire in her parlour, washing them down with a large cup of Mrs. Meggott's strong, sweet tea.

"To think that less than a week ago you was sitting here with that other young lady. Poor thing. And her carrying on about what she knew and could tell the police if she was so minded. What do you think it was, miss?"

"I don't know, Mrs. Meggott."

"Well, even if you did I wouldn't blame you for keeping it to yourself," said the worthy woman rather unexpectedly. "Least said soonest mended and especially to the police. I'm law abiding, and always have been, but I don't hold with getting mixed up in such doings and the police are a nosy lot. If you ask me, miss, I think young Doris over at Scanbridge could have done better than that Welsh cop she's walking out with, and her aunt Emily shouldn't have encouraged it."

"The police are well paid," said Cherry, "and they get pensions."

Mrs. Meggott, who liked to know all that was going on, showed no sign of going back to her kitchen but remained solidly planted in the doorway. "I did hear it said he'd been told off to look after you like," she remarked, "but you've shook him off to-day seemingly. I reckon he could hardly come along to school with you like Mary's little lamb."

"I wonder how you heard that."

"My old father was down to Emily's with some green stuff off his allotment and saw Evan Griffiths there, and her pampering him up with sausages. I hope Emily makes you comfortable, miss?"

"Oh, quite."

"Well, those high-up cops from the Yard have been staying at the Green Man and throwing their weight about, but it doesn't look as if they was going to arrest anybody. If you ask me it was somebody who came down from London for the purpose who did in that Greville person, and it was no more than she deserved, the—well, I won't demean myself nor soil my lips by saying what she was— and back he went where he come from, and who's to find him among all those millions."

Cherry wanted to say that Mrs. Meggott's theory left Betty Haydon's murder unexplained, but she knew by experience that she was not amenable to argument when once she had made up her mind.

Mrs. Meggott seemed to have more to say, but she was recalled to her kitchen by an unmistakable smell of burning pastry and prevented from returning by the arrival of various members of her large family coming in for their mid-day meal.

The afternoon school began at two. Cherry smoked a cigarette and waited until five minutes before the hour, and then went back. Some of the other students were there before her, and they made room for her where they were sitting round the stove as they had never done before. If they went on being friendly, she thought, the rest of the term might be just bearable. She began to realise dimly that poor Betty had not been liked and that she had shared her unpopularity because they had always been together.

Kent did not visit the Prelim at all during the afternoon. Old Stryver had left at three as he often did, alleging that he had to feed his pigs, and during the last hour the students had drawn from casts. At four o'clock the school bell rang.

There was the usual rush for the lockers and then for the dressing-rooms. No one tried to dispute possession of the one small discoloured mirror with the glamorous Gertie and two or three others who were admittedly what Rossetti and his friends would have called stunners. Cherry got her coat and her beret from her hook and slipped away unnoticed.

Normally the wintry dusk would have been brightened by the glow of firelight shining through cottage panes and the red blinds of the Green Man. As it was, doors were being closed and curtains drawn to hide the faintest gleam, and the dispersing students vanished like shadows. Cherry found herself looking forward with nervous anticipation to the mile of open road between the village and the cottages near the station where she lodged. It was on her way to and fro to school that she was going to miss Betty most, and it was of the dead girl that she was thinking as she passed the garden gate of the last cottage.

Had Betty known fear before she died? Had she seen the hand with the knife—

There was a sudden stealthy movement on the farther side of the hedge that screened the fields from the road. Cherry started violently, and then laughed at herself. It was only a cow or perhaps a horse cropping the grass. It was still light enough to see a large animal moving. A small boy who had been swinging on a garden gate bobbed up suddenly at her elbow.

"Hi, miss—"

"Yes. What is it?"

"Are you Miss Garth?"

"Yes."

"I was to say will you go back to the school, please? Will you go back and wait in Mr. Kent's room?"

"Oh—" The dark world blazed up for Cherry with red and blue stars and lovely showers of golden rain. Her heart seemed to turn over in her breast. Then she had not been mistaken after all. He would not send her such a message if he did not—did not want her.

"Oh, my darling," sang Cherry's heart, as she hurried back the way she had come.

She met one farm labourer who wished her a gruff good night as he passed her. The small boy had vanished. Nobody saw her unlatch the school gate and walk quickly up the rough road to the main building. She was only just visible in the fast gathering darkness and the only people who might have stopped her, the caretaker and his wife, were just sitting down to their tea and had turned the wireless on.

"You haven't locked up yet," said Mrs. Pearce.

Pearce had started on his kipper and he answered with his mouth full. "You said Mr. Kent's going to be working late. He'll lock up and drop the keys in our letter-box on his way out."

"I suppose that's all right," said his wife doubtfully. "We've had trouble enough."

"That's what you think," growled the caretaker. "The students will stay till the end of the term because they've paid their fees and want their money's worth. But they won't come back after this shemozzle. You and me'll be looking for a job. Our home and our living gone, and all because of that—"

Mrs. Pearce cut short his description of the late Althea Greville. "That'll do, Tom," she said with a shudder. "She's dead. What's that?"

"What? Atmospherics, I expect." He got up and twiddled the knobs of the wireless.

At Bello Sguardo, too, the wireless was blaring. Beppi had got an Italian station and was listening to a programme of operatic records while he cleaned the silver. He was alone in the house, for Morosini had rung up to say he was remaining in London. Lady Violet had changed her mind again, and she and her friend were dining with him at the Ritz and going to a show afterwards.

The main hall of the school building was dark when Cherry went in. She stood for a moment, waiting, hoping to hear Kent's voice saying, "Here you are. I knew you wouldn't fail me—" but the silence remained unbroken.

She was afraid to switch on a light in case it showed outside.

She made her way across the hall, past the door of the office, which was shut, and that of the preliminary classroom, which had been left open. The familiar smell of turpentine and cigarette smoke was reassuring, but the casts ranged round the walls glimmered like sheeted ghosts and gave her an eerie feeling that they had just moved and would be moving again as soon as her back was turned. She bit her lip hard. It was silly to be frightened. It was quite early really, but these November days were so short.

She hurried on down the long corridor, trying not to think of the life classroom on the other side which had been unused since the model had been murdered there, less than a week ago.

Her first glow of happy confidence was fading and she was beginning to ask herself why he wanted to see her like this secretly and alone. Why hadn't he asked her when he paused by her easel earlier in the day, instead of sending her a message through one of the village children? It was queer, but there must, she knew, be some good reason for everything he did.

This was his room. Again she waited, screwing up her courage before she knocked.

"It's me. Cherry—"

She was not sure if he replied, but there was some sound within, and she turned the knob and entered. To her surprise the room was as dark as the corridor. For a moment as she moved forward uncertainly, she thought she had been mistaken and that there was nobody there, and then as she paused, a floor-board creaked just behind her and with that sound came a cold crawling horror and the conviction that she was in imminent danger.

Some obscure instinct prompted her to move sideways instead of forward, and a glancing blow all but missed her and merely brushed her shoulder. It was sheer luck that her hand found the door-knob without an instant's delay, but as she ran down the corridor she knew that she was being followed. She turned into the preliminary class-room and slammed the door. As she leant against it she felt the knob turning in spite of her efforts to hold it, and a pressure being exerted to force it open, which she was not strong enough to withstand.

Her only hope was that she might outwit her pursuer. She sprang back and the ensuing crash told her that he had been taken by surprise and had lost his balance. There were further crashes as she knocked over an easel and a plaster cast. Then—after a momentary silence—heavy footsteps and heavy breathing and scuffling and creaking sounds as chairs and easels were thrust aside by hands that groped in the dark.

CHAPTER XIX
THE CLUE OF THE FOOTPRINTS

CHERRY'S landlady opened the door a few inches. "Who is it, please?"

"Detective-Inspector Collier and Sergeant Duffield. I want to see Constable Griffiths."

"He isn't here."

"Not here? I think you had better let us in, Miss Tremlett—"

"Very well."

When the door was closed she turned up the gas jet in the tiny hall and led the way into the front sitting-room, where a cloth was laid for Cherry's tea.

"I was expecting Miss Garth any minute," she explained. "She's a bit later than usual."

"Griffiths has gone up to the school to see her home, I suppose?"

"No, he hasn't, Inspector. He's gone back to Scanbridge. They are understaffed there, owing to so many being down with the 'flu."

Collier stared at her. "Do you mean that he was recalled—that he had orders to return?"

"That's what I understood, certainly."

"Has Mr. Kent been here again since he called the other day?"

"No, he hasn't. Evan was afraid he'd get into trouble over that, but Miss Garth was all for letting him in, and Evan made them leave the door of this room open and he stayed in the passage, and we could hear every word that was said as we sat having our tea in the kitchen and it seemed harmless enough."

"Can you remember what they talked about?"

"About the murders and especially about Miss Garth's friend that was killed at the pictures. Well, there, I can't bear to think of it. And as to going to the cinema alone after this—"

"Was there anything about the possibility of Betty Haydon having passed on what she knew to someone else?"

"Yes. I remember Miss Garth saying that she talked a lot to her aunt's maid and that she might have told her, and that she might be able to help the police. And soon after that Mr. Kent took his leave, and that very evening she was found at the foot of the cellar stairs. My neighbour's eldest boy works over at Scanminster and he says it's made a lot of talk over there, and no wonder. Oh—" her eyes widened and her hand went up to her mouth. It was clear that she had just realised a possible connection between hitherto unrelated facts. "You don't think—"

"That conversation you overheard may be important," said Collier patiently. "You and Griffiths can bear witness to what was said. Was there anyone else in the kitchen at the time who could corroborate your account?"

"There was my niece Gladys and old Mr. Stryver, who had brought me some greens from his allotment," Miss Tremlett said eagerly.

Collier looked at his watch. He was frowning.

"The students come out at four. What time does Miss Garth come in as a rule?"

"Round about half-past. She's very late—"

Collier caught Duffield's eye. "I think we'll get going. Thank you, Miss Tremlett."

"I don't like this," said Collier, as he turned the car to go back to the village. "Why the hell did Pearson take that Welsh fellow off? He might at least have let me know. I'll admit I did say I thought the danger would be over when she'd given her evidence at the inquest. The trouble is that we all have to make two men do the work of five nowadays. We can't spread ourselves as we did in peace time. This damned black-out. We may pass her along the road—"

"Shall I walk? There's only the one footpath?"

"That's an idea. If you meet her take her back to her lodgings and then join me. I'm going to the school."

He stopped the car at the school gate. The fine drizzle that had begun to fall at dusk had turned to heavy continuous rain. He was hardly surprised that he had to knock three times at the door of the caretaker's cottage before Mrs. Pearce came to open it.

"Is that you, Mr. Kent, sir?"

"No. Were you expecting Mr. Kent?"

"He was working late and was to leave the keys as he went home."

"I'll be seeing him then. I'm going up to the school. Where's your husband?"

"Finishing his tea. Did you want him?"

"Yes. He'd better come with me. Tell him to put on his waterproof if he's got one. It's raining cats and dogs."

"Won't you come in, Inspector? He's in his slippers and he'll have to put on his boots. Pearce can't risk catching a cold, not with his chest."

"Very well."

She showed him into the chilly, overcrowded front parlour and left him there. In the kitchen Pearce was filling his pipe. He was pale, and his sunken eyes had the hunted, expression that had troubled her when he first came home after the war from the hospital where he had been treated for shell-shock.

"Tom—"

"The—the cops again?" She was horrified to see that his lips were trembling.

"Tom. For God's sake—you haven't done nothing wrong? Oh, Tom—"

"No. Of course not. It's just—my nerves."

"He only wants you to go up to the school with him," she faltered.

"No, Annie. I can't."

"Tom!" She went up to him and laid a hand on his arm. "Pull yourself together like. If you act queer he's bound to think—Tom, I'll stick to you through thick and thin. I always have, haven't I?"

He swallowed hard. "Very well. Tell him I'm coming." He sat down and reached for his boots under the chair.

Mrs. Pearce went back to the parlour. "He won't be a minute, Inspector."

Collier was standing. He had been turning over the pages of a large family Bible that lay on a red wool mat on a table in the window, with a pink and blue vase inscribed, 'A Present from Margate", which Pearce had won as a prize in the shooting gallery of a fun fair, and an aspidistra in a pot, wrapped up in crepe tissue paper.

"Don't worry, Mrs. Pearce," he said with what was, to her, an unexpected gentleness.

She stared back at him dumbly, her work-worn hands fumbling at the folds of her apron, until her husband called to them from the passage that he was ready.

"Sorry to take you out in this downpour," said Collier, as they trudged up the drive together. Pearce made no reply, but when they reached the main building he asked if he should go in first and turn on the light in the hall.

"Yes, please."

Collier heard the switch, click, but the light did not come on.

"Must have fused," muttered Pearce.

"Try the one in the office."

"I can't get in there. Mr. Kent keeps it locked since the secretary left, and he has the key. Wait a bit. There's another switch for the corridor."

He tried again, with the same result.

"Must have fused all over. But Mr. Kent hasn't brought over the keys. He can't be working in the dark—" Pearce sounded puzzled.

"Can the light be turned off at the meter?"

"Yes. But who would do that?"

"Never mind. Find out. Where is the meter?"

"In the cupboard where I keep my brooms. You stop where you are, and I'll see. You may be right. It's queer—God! What was that!"

There was a deafening crash. The sound seemed to come from the preliminary classroom. Collier rushed across the hall and reached the doorway at the same moment as the caretaker. This time the light came on as he touched the switch.

The large room was filled with a cloud of fine white dust through which loomed a wreckage of overturned chairs and easels and the shattered limbs and bodies of plaster casts from the antique.

"What the hell's been going on here?" cried Pearce. "Inspector—" his voice cracked. "Is that an animal?"

"No, no—"

The man who had emerged from the midst of the slowly subsiding cloud of plaster dust rose from his hands and knees and staggered towards them. It was old Stryver, his face, his hair, his clothing all white, so that he had an uncanny look of one of the casts coming to life.

"Thank the Lord you've come," he croaked. "I heard a noise and summat fell on me—" he broke off to cough.

They both stared at him, and Pearce said sharply, "What were you doing here?"

"I come back for my baccy pouch. It must ha' dropped out of my coat pocket when I was sitting for my picture this afternoon."

"You were looking for it in the dark?"

"I tried the light, but it wouldn't go on."

"Was the room in this state when you came in?"

"I couldn't see in the dark," he said in an injured tone, "but I barked my shins something cruel on summat, and then there was a noise like the end of the world and I kind of lost count of things. Must have passed out, I reckon. And now this damned stuff is stinging my nose and eyes—"

"All right," said Collier curtly. "You stop with him here by the door, Pearce, while I have a look round."

His own throat was irritated by the all-pervading white dust and his eyes were watering, but much of it had settled and it was now possible to see across the room. Several of the casts that had formerly been ranged around the walls were now lying in fragments on the floor. He noticed that the chairs and easels that had been thrown over were unbroken. There must have been numerous crashes before the last one which they had heard. He glanced round at the old man, who was leaning weakly against the wall and wiping his face with a dingy bandanna handkerchief.

"I wonder you didn't fall over some of these bits and pieces as you came in."

"Nearly did, I reckon."

Collier picked his way among the wreckage to the far side of the room.

"Miss Garth—"

Cherry crept out from her dusty hiding-place behind the dancing faun, stumbled into his arms and burst out crying with the loud, uncontrolled sobs of a frightened child.

Collier patted her on the back. "That's all right. You're quite safe now—" His voice was gentle, but his eyes were hard as steel. "What happened?"

"I—I—oh—"

"Never mind." He looked towards the door. The sergeant and Kent had just come in together and were gazing in amazement at the devastation. He led Cherry towards them, keeping one arm about her.

Kent started forward. His face was white. "Cherry. What's been going on here? You're not hurt—"

Duffield looked for a lead to his superior officer. Collier nodded and a ham-like hand descended on the art master's shoulder.

"Just a minute, sir, if you please," said Duffield, in the official voice that was oddly unlike his usual good-humoured manner.

Kent opened his mouth to protest, and shut it again without saying anything.

"Now, Miss Garth," said Collier persuasively, "if you could tell us, as clearly as possible, what has been happening here and why, it would save a lot more trouble. Try, there's a good girl. Pearce, bring her a chair, and you might fetch a glass of water—"

Cherry's knees were knocking together and she was thankful to sit down. She fumbled in vain for her handkerchief, and finally accepted a large square of cambric from Collier. The water was brought, and she drank while they stood round her in a semi-circle.

"Why didn't you leave the school at four o'clock with the other students, Miss Garth?"

"I did."

"Why did you come back then?"

There was a pause. Cherry smoothed her tweed skirt down over her knees with trembling fingers. She had lost her beret and her hair was rumpled and hanging over her face. Her coat and her frock were smeared with plaster dust and grime and cobwebs. Tears had made channels in the dust on her round cheeks.

"A—a boy stopped me as I was going down the road. He said Mr. Kent wanted to speak to me and that he—he was waiting in his room at the school, so—so I came back."

"What happened then?"

"I went to his room and knocked. I don't know if there was an answer, but when I went in it was dark; I—I couldn't understand it. I was frightened. Then something—someone—came up behind me. I got away. I ran down the passage and in here. I shut the door, but the key was on the other side. He had followed and was pushing to get in. He was stronger than I was. All this time neither of us had said a word. I let go and he fell in. I threw things down, hoping that the noise would confuse him and I got into a corner and hid behind one of the casts. He tried to switch on the light but it didn't go on. I heard him creeping about trying to find me. Oh, it was horrible. It seemed like hours and hours, but perhaps it was only a few minutes. Now and then he fell against things or knocked something over and made a frightful din, but the last was the worst. I think it was one of the bigger casts. And then the lights went on and I heard voices, but I couldn't see anything where I was, and I was afraid to move—"

"Thank you. Miss Garth. Now, Mr. Kent, if you care to make a statement? I must warn you though that anything you say may be used in evidence—"

"I don't understand this," said Kent. "I didn't send Miss Garth any message—about waiting for her in my room, I mean. I never thought of such a thing. I went home as usual a little before four, and had tea. I came out again, as a matter of fact, with some idea of calling on Miss Garth at her lodgings and I met the sergeant just outside the school gate. He asked me to come in with him."

The caretaker seemed about to speak, but Collier stopped him. "Just a moment, Pearce. I think I know what you were going to say. We'll come to that presently. When you came in here, Stryver, some of the chairs had been knocked over and the casts thrown down? Or would you say the damage was done after you arrived?"

"Some of it before, I reckon," said the old man doubtfully. "I couldn't swear to it though."

"You didn't hear any sound as you entered the building?"

"Come to think of it, I did. But I didn't pay no attention. I thought it might be Pearce breaking up coal for the stoves."

"I was at home having my tea," said Pearce defensively.

"You have heard what Miss Garth has told us, Stryver. Think back now. Did you hear any sound that might have been made by her assailant as he got by you and escaped?"

Stryver scratched his frowsy grey head reflectively.

"Can't say I did. He must have got away under cover of that big noise."

"Look here—" began Kent excitedly, but Collier held up his hand.

"You'll have a chance to explain. Sergeant, will you take Stryver out to the car. We shall have to run you down to Scanbridge, Stryver, to take down your statement. You'll have it read over to you before you sign it."

"Won't to-morrow do?" growled Stryver. "I want to get home to my tea. I got a pork chop to fry, and the cat'll be getting at it—"

"They'll be able to give you a cup of tea and bread and butter at the station," said Collier consolingly. "I can't promise a pork chop, I'm afraid. All right, Duffield. I'll join you in a minute."

The old man shambled out reluctantly, grumbling to himself, and the burly sergeant followed.

As soon as the door closed behind them Collier turned to the caretaker. "What were you going to say just now?"

"I was going to ask Mr. Kent if he didn't tell my wife that he would be working late and that he'd drop the keys of the school in our letter-box as he passed out?"

"No," said Kent. "I didn't. I went home a little before four and got my own tea. My sister and her son were out, so you'll have to take my word for it. My God! I suppose I can't prove that I wasn't here creeping about in the dark and trying to murder you, Cherry."

Cherry said nothing, but she made a little unconscious movement towards him, and a little colour came into her pale cheeks under the disfiguring streaks of grime and plaster.

"Mrs. Pearce was here at the school this afternoon then?" said Collier.

"No, she wasn't. She was at home doing her washing. She always puts it out Mondays, rain or shine."

"What opportunity did she have to get this alleged message to you from Mr. Kent? Be careful, Pearce. This is important."

"Why, she had it from Stryver. I remember now. She was hanging out a sheet and he come down the drive from the school. It was round about half-past three. He stopped to speak to her, and when she came in she told me Mr. Kent was working late and that he'd lock up."

"I don't get this," said Kent. "I sent no message through Stryver or anyone else."

"That's all right, sir," said Collier. "It's all coming along very nicely."

Kent stared at him. "I don't understand. You can't really tell who ran amuck in here, can you?"

"Can't I? The murderer has been clever, but he slipped up to-night. Miss Garth looks all in, and no wonder. Perhaps you will see her home, Mr. Kent?"

"You aren't going to arrest me then?"

Collier smiled and glanced at the girl. "What do you say, Miss Garth?"

He read gratitude in her eyes. "Of course not." She took Kent's arm. "Please, John—"

CHAPTER XX
THE CASE IS OVER

AT HALF-PAST six the superintendent of police at Scanbridge telephoned to the Chief Constable, who lived in one of the fine old Georgian houses in the High Street, not five minutes' walk from the station. Major Payne, after hearing what he had to say, cancelled a dinner engagement, and hurried over.

He found the two detectives from the Yard and his superintendent in the latter's room. The superintendent was obviously worried, but he could not read the faces of the other two.

"I understand that you've made an arrest—burnt your boats—and that it isn't Kent? Are you quite sure of your ground, Inspector? I confess I'm astounded. I thought we were all certain that Kent was our man."

"I have not charged anybody with murder—yet—" said Collier mildly. "I am asking you to detain Albert Stryver pending enquiries. Perhaps I had better tell you what happened this afternoon."

"Yes. Yes, of course."

Major Payne and his superintendent listened carefully to Collier's account of what had been going on at the school. When he had done they looked at each other and the superintendent voiced the thought of both. "I don't see how this let's the master out. Why, from what you tell us the evidence against him is overwhelming."

Collier shook his head. "Don't you see, it's too much. It's phoney. Is it likely that a man who had planned to meet a girl in an empty building, intending to murder her, would make the appointment through one of the village boys, and warn the caretaker that he would be on the spot, working late, and locking up when his job was done? Kent wasn't in the clear, he never had an alibi, but I believe that was just bad luck until to-day. This time, I'm certain, he was being framed. It nearly came off, too. If I had not visited the school after hours, Cherry Garth's body would have been found to-morrow morning. The Pearces and Stryver would have given their evidence about the late working and the keys dropped in the letter-box—and, in the case of the Pearces, they would have sworn a man's life away in perfect good faith. The only hope that justice might still be done would have depended on the size of Kent's feet."

Major Payne stared. "I don't quite follow—"

"When we entered that classroom the air was thick with white dust, the plaster of the broken casts. And not only the air. It had settled on everything and lay thick on the floor. The dust showed me that Stryver was lying when he tried to make us believe that he had only just arrived and that Miss Garth's assailant was there and got by him in the dark. The only footprints in the dust were his own, weaving in and out among the overturned chairs and easels. Cherry Garth's were there, but only from the corner where she had hidden to the door, and then mine were beside hers. If, however, we had not come when we did much would have depended on whether it was possible to identify the footprints. Stryver was not wearing the heavy hobnailed boots one would have expected. I noticed that his shoes, though old and worn, were of a good make. Probably they were given to him, and quite possibly by Kent, who engaged him to sit for the students, and saw him every day. In any case, if their feet were the same size, the prints would merely have confused us. As it is, most fortunately, they provide us with irrefutable evidence against one man, and that man is Stryver."

Major Payne took off his glasses and polished them on his handkerchief. "Who is this man? This is the first I've heard of him."

"He lives alone in a cottage on the outskirts of the village, and picks up a living here and there, doing odd jobs, selling the green stuff from his allotment, and posing for the students at the Morosini School. His married daughter is a Mrs. Meggott who keeps a sweetshop and sells teas and minerals. Miss Garth and her friend, Betty Haydon, sometimes had lunch there, and we've always supposed that Betty's boasts of what she knew and could tell were overheard and cost her her life."

"But the motive for the first murder—" began the Major.

"I think I've got that," said Collier, "but I'm going to question him now and perhaps he may tell us himself. Would you care to be present, Major? We've kept him waiting a bit. It usually has a good effect."

"Very well," said the Chief Constable, "but for heaven's sake be careful, Inspector. Remember Judge's Rules. No third degree stuff."

Collier smiled and looked across at the superintendent, who rang a bell, and told the young constable who answered it to bring Stryver in to them.

Stryver had gruffly declined the offer of a wash and brush up, but he had wiped most of the plaster off his face with a grimy handkerchief. His rosy cheeks, blue eyes, and grey chin whiskers normally gave him the air of a stage rustic, a picturesque old gaffer hobbling about leaning on a stick, but a closer inspection corrected this first impression and gave it a slightly sinister twist. The shaven lips were drawn down at the corners, the little eyes under the grey penthouse brows were needle sharp, stabbing here and there. He sat down unasked and glowered at Collier.

"Plenty of time to waste hereabouts, seemingly," he said sourly. "Mine's valuable. What about my fowls?"

"I just want to run through that statement of yours over again," explained Collier. "It will be taken down and read over to you." He glanced across at the constable who sat outside the circle of lamplight with his fountain pen and his writing block. "Just give it to us in your own words. You went back to the school to find your tobacco pouch, which you thought you might have dropped on the model's throne. Is that right?"

"Ar." Slowly and with frequent pauses for thought, Stryver repeated his former statement almost word for word to a silent and attentive audience.

"That's all," he said finally, preparing to rise. "I reckon I don't have to tell you who it was up to his tricks. Mr. Kent, he's your man. If I'd ha' been you I'd have took him while I had him under my hand as it were, and perhaps you did, but I haven't seen him here, nor heard his voice. You cops had better look out he don't slip through your fingers. Am I to be took home in a car or do I get my bus fare?"

"Neither," said Collier blandly, "you're staying here." Stryver half rose from his chair. Nobody moved or spoke. His little eyes flickered as he sat down again.

"What for?" His voice had thickened and lost some of its assurance.

"Have you a pencil, Stryver?"

"I—yes—what about it?"

"Will you let me see it?"

Stryver hesitated, and then, after some fumbling in his coat pockets, produced a stub. Collier took it from him and tried it on a sheet of paper on the superintendent's desk.

"Blue indelible. You used it the last time you took flowers to your son's grave, didn't you, to write on the base of the monument, Ezekiel xvi. 41, 42, 43? I only saw it this afternoon, but I was able to look up the reference in Pearce's Bible before we went along to the school."

The other men in the room, watching Stryver, saw his colour fade to a sickly yellow and beads of sweat start out on his forehead and his upper lip.

"I copied all three verses in my notebook," said Collier. "Here they are. 'And they shall burn thine houses with fire and execute judgments upon thee in the sight of many women: and I will cause thee to cease from playing the harlot, and thou shalt give no hire any more. So will I make my fury towards thee to rest, and my jealousy shall depart from thee, and I will be quiet, and will no more be angry. Because thou hast not remembered the days of thy youth, but hast fretted me in all these things, behold, I also will recompense thy way upon thy head, saith the Lord God.' That was the morning after the murder of Althea Greville, wasn't it?"

There was a long silence.

Collier, looking at that narrow, stubborn face, the face of a ruthless fanatic, but without the saving grace of selflessness that sometimes ennobles the type, waited patiently.

Would the breakdown come now, or must he go on?

Stryver swallowed hard, and moistened his dry lips. He was aware of the strained attention of all those present.

He was important, wasn't he. All these cops, some of them high up—

His subconscious mind, gliding over the fact that he was lost, prepared a new attitude that would maintain his self-respect and soothe his vanity.

He said, "All right. I'll tell you. She killed my boy, see. My Bert. He was my youngest. He come long after the others and his mother died when he was born. A good boy he was and good at his books. Won a scholarship, he did, and come over to the High School. A nice-looking young chap he was, and got a place in a house agents' office. Quite the gentleman. But he lived along of me and wasn't ashamed of his old dad. I had to help him out, see, for he didn't get much wages, not so much as if he'd done rough work, but I didn't mind that. I was proud of him. And then, last summer, that woman was staying in the village while she worked at the school, and she turned several of the young chaps' heads, and my Bert's among them. I didn't know what was going on at the time or where he went evenings, but later I found out. He took money from his employers to spend on her, and though they didn't prosecute they gave him the sack. And when she'd gone he saw she'd only been carrying on with him to amuse herself, and that she didn't care a snap of her fingers for him. I tried to talk him out of it, but he wouldn't listen to me. He got very quiet, and one evening I come home from work and I found him hanging in the shed behind my cottage. Twenty years old, he was, and lovely bright hair, like corn. There was an inquest and they brought it in temp'rary insanity, but I knew she'd murdered him just as much as if she'd stuck a knife into him, and I thought to myself 'If we meet again, my lady, you'll pay.' And I got my savings and I bought him a nice angel and a marble kerb, but I couldn't make up my mind about a text, so I told them to leave a space and maybe I'd choose one later on. And when she came back here I thought, 'The Lord has delivered her into my hands.' It was easy, and nobody would have seen me if that Haydon girl hadn't come back for her scarf. I stepped back pretty quick, and I wasn't sure if she'd noticed me, but the next day I was having a bit of dinner at my daughter's place, and she was in the parlour with her friend and I heard her going on about what she knew and what she could tell. I never liked her. Always complaining that I didn't keep the pose. A nosy little bitch. I felt I shouldn't be safe while she was about. And then the next day I was in Scanbridge and I saw her going into the Picture House. She was alone, and it seemed the best chance I should get. I got behind her and finished her off without saying a word and got out while the chap in the posh uniform was looking the other way, and walked home. I was too sharp for the lot of you there, I reckon; but still I wasn't easy in my mind in case she might have blabbed to somebody, after all. And then, when I was over at my niece Emily Tremlett's house with some greens I'd pulled for her, I found that there Welsh chap young Doris is walking out with on guard like, and Mr. Kent had come to see that other girl, the little round-faced one, and we heard them talking, and saying Betty might have talked to her aunt's servant, Emma Price. I was forced to laugh," said old Stryver, with a cackle that sounded strangely inhuman to his hearers in that quiet room. "Emma and me was young together, and left school and went to work about the same time. I got taken on at the butcher's in the High Street at Scanminster, and she was in a place there. I was sweet on her, but she wouldn't have me because she didn't fancy the butchering and couldn't bear the thought of me with blood on my hands, or some such foolishness. I hadn't seen her for years, but I knew she was with that Miss Haydon in one of them terrace houses near the cathedral, so I thought I'd go over and make sure she didn't do me a mischief. Them old maids can be spiteful. That was a mess up though. A bell rang just as she opened the side door, and I was afraid it was Miss Haydon and that if it wasn't answered quick she'd use her latchkey, so I just shoved Emma down the cellar steps, but I didn't make a thorough job of it."

He had got over the shock of realising that he had been found out, and had regained his colour, only his coarse, earth-stained hands still shook slightly as he fumbled at the brim of his hat. His listeners were all too accustomed to the workings of the criminal mind to be surprised at his complete lack of feeling for his victims.

Major Payne said curtly, "Don't let that worry you, Stryver. Emma Price died in hospital this afternoon."

"Ar," said the lover of her girlhood complacently. "Cracked her skull, I reckon. Poor old Emma. Well, you read that over to me and I'll sign it. I'd just like to ask one thing."

"What is that?"

His cunning little eyes darted from face to face, swift as the flicker of a snake's tongue.

"I'd like a nice fat pork chop for my supper."

"Good God!" muttered the Chief Constable, but he nodded at his superintendent, who answered the prisoner in the cool impersonal tones of officialdom, "We'll see what can be done."

EPILOGUE

ONE afternoon some months later, Inspector Collier was about to cross Victoria Street when a girl in the uniform of the W.A.A.F. came up to him.

"Oh, please—I'm so glad to see you. John and I want to thank you—" she said breathlessly.

For a moment he could not place her, and then he realised that it was Cherry Garth. She looked very well, and the blue of her smartly-fitted Service coat became her round rosy cheeks and shining brown curls.

"John—" he said, smiling.

A voice behind him joined in. "That's me. May I introduce my wife, Inspector."

"Fine, Mr. Kent," said Collier heartily. "I hoped that would happen." He shook hands with them both, touched by their evident pleasure in the chance meeting.

"You'll come and have a cup of tea with us," urged Cherry, "there's a nice quiet place just here."

When they were settled at a corner table and tea had been ordered, he had time to notice how much younger and more spruce Kent appeared in his R.A.F. uniform. But he still had the same hesitating and diffident manner. "I don't go up, you know," he explained. "Too old, and all that. Actually, I have rather a hush hush job as a draughtsman."

They talked about themselves for a while, and then Kent referred to the trial at which they had both been called as witnesses for the Crown.

"What did you think of the verdict, guilty but insane?"

"He was sane enough," said Collier, "but the counsel's speech for the defence worked on the jury's feelings. The heart-broken father and so on. He was a cunning old devil and nearly got away with it. Between ourselves, Mr. Kent, until nearly the end of the case, I thought Pearce, the caretaker, was our man. He made a bad impression. Sheer nerves, I suppose."

"And a guilty conscience," said Kent. "You know the students complained of the pilfering that was going on. There was some idea of setting a trap, and I fancy that poor Betty Haydon thought she had spotted the thief when she saw Stryver in the school after hours. Actually Pearce was the culprit. He confessed to me before he left at the end of the term. It was partly his wife's fault. She handled his wages and doled out a shilling or two now and then. And like most old soldiers he has a craving for tobacco. Well, he's had his lesson and has sworn to go straight in future. I got him a job through a friend of mine and so far there have been no complaints."

"The Morosini School has closed down for good?"

"For the duration anyway. And I doubt if Morosini will reopen it. Collier, I've been hoping we might meet again like this unofficially," said Kent earnestly. "We did want to thank you, as Cherry said just now, and we didn't get a chance during the trial. We both realise that we owe you our lives. That last night—I shudder to think what would have happened if you had not turned up when you did. You saved us."

"Yes, you saved us," Cherry echoed him.

Collier was pleased, but so much gratitude was embarrassing. He looked at his watch. "Heavens! I must fly—"

"We'll meet again after the war."

"After the war."

They went up together to the street level.

"Cheerio. All the best."

"Cheerio."

They shook hands again, and then John and Cherry climbed on to a bus, and Collier walked on to the Yard.

THE END

Printed in Germany
by Amazon Distribution
GmbH, Leipzig

17591829R00123